A WINNING HAND

A Novel

By

Alexandra Y. Caluen

A WINNING HAND
Copyright 2020 by Alexandra Y. Caluen
All Rights Reserved

Cover design by RK Young

Cover photo by Mathew Schwartz @cadop
unsplash.com

A WINNING HAND

The Playlist:

Are You Lonesome Tonight? – Frank Sinatra

Danke Schöen – Wayne Newton

Poker Face – Lady Gaga

The Gambler – Kenny Rogers

The Name of the Game – ABBA

Let's Start Tomorrow Tonight – Leslie Odom Jr.

Viva Las Vegas – Elvis Presley

Gimme Shelter – Rolling Stones

Lady Luck – Brian Setzer Orchestra

Let It Ride – Charlie Clouser

The Game - Queen

A WINNING HAND

Contents

I - Lou

August 2015

When I got the call I thought *hell*, because it was a domestic disturbance. Those had quickly become my least favorite. So rarely resolved in any true sense of the word, and so often merely one in a string of gradually-escalating events. I'd been with the Las Vegas Police Department for a little over three years, and I'd already seen four of these cases come to bad conclusions: a parent injured or dead, children traumatized, and someone going to prison.

I pulled in a minute behind Dominguez, the officer who'd called for backup. We went up to the apartment in the usual way, ready for anything. We could hear a man and woman yelling at each other inside. Dominguez gave me a nod; I unholstered my weapon to cover him. He knocked.

We heard the man say, "Oh now the fucking neighbors have to get involved."

The woman said, "If you weren't such a won't-take-no asshole nobody would be involved." Her voice got louder, obviously approaching the door. She opened it. "Oh."

From there it was the usual, if less fraught than the usual. There weren't any kids, and the only sign of violence was on the guy. It was a mark on his ribs that would be a bruise in a few hours, and he wasn't proud of it. The only reason he showed us was I noticed him rubbing it. He said she hit him, she admitted it, and then we had to find out why.

Dominguez talked to her while I talked to the guy. Yes, they had a relationship. No, he didn't live there. A

1

show of embarrassment about being so loud, a surprisingly unconvincing apology for troubling us. Assurance that it wouldn't happen again.

She heard him. "Damn right it won't. I want him out of here."

"What? Gloria, come on."

"Go home. Don't come back. Don't call me." She wasn't looking at him. She was staring at Dominguez. "He has a key. Please get it from him."

Dominguez glanced at me. This was unusual. The woman, Gloria Louise Bartolo according to what she'd said, was sitting at her little table wrapped in a casino-branded spa robe. "Where did you get that robe, Ms. Bartolo?"

I saw her face change from exhaustion, annoyance, and well-hidden fear to cold blankness. A face that said okay, so this is a complete waste of time. "It was a gift from my boss," she said, clearly expecting him not to believe her.

He frowned a little, because he didn't. Stolen spa robes were all over the place in LV. I said, "She works for the casino." Dominguez looked at me again; I nodded; he nodded and moved on. Bartolo was looking at me now, probably wondering how I knew that. There was only one way, of course. I'd seen her perform. She played piano for Gino Corsetti's Sinatra tribute show.

Dominguez said, "Both of you please stay where you are for a minute." They didn't move. Either they had some experience with police, or they didn't want to get any. Dominguez and I gave them as much space as possible. He spoke very quietly. "She says he wanted to do something, she told him no, it escalated. What does he say?"

"Same thing except some whining. He says they've been going out for a year or so."

"Did he say when he got a key?"

"Didn't ask. If she wants it back, let's get it back. Did she say what he wanted to do?"

"Only said it was something she didn't want to do. Did he say?"

I nodded. The guy had obviously – to me – thought he was entitled to whatever he wanted. I'd run up against that a few too many times. "Said he wanted the back door."

Dominguez made a face like 'is that all?' He stared over at both of them for a few seconds until he had their full attention. "Mr. Samuels, why did this escalate to the point that we were called."

"It was ridiculous." It was like he forgot we were cops, he was so eager to justify himself. "It's not like we haven't done it before."

"Is that true, Ms. Bartolo?"

"Does it matter?" she snapped. And of course it didn't. I was annoyed Dominguez asked that, but not as annoyed as she was. "Maybe you want the details, Officer? No prep, no lube, and no condom, that's what he wanted, and he tried to hold me down to do it." Her voice wasn't shaking but her hands were.

I made a move. Dominguez saw me. He nodded again. "Do you want to press charges?"

She rolled her eyes. "What would be the point?" And, sadly, she was right. Samuels looked relieved anyway. Bartolo said, "Just please get him out of here. Get his stuff out of here. Get my key. Thank you."

Dominguez and I made eye contact again. He said, "Mr. Samuels, the key." The guy made a huffy noise, but dug in his pocket, pulled out a bunch of keys, and detached one. Dominguez took it and showed it to Bartolo. "Is this the key?" She nodded. He handed it to her. "Mr. Samuels, let's go."

"What about my stuff?"

"Officer Kravitz will get it." He didn't take hold of Samuels, but the guy did a fair perp walk anyway.

When I was alone with Gloria Louise, I said, "Are you all right, ma'am?"

She took a deep breath and slowly exhaled. "I'm feeling very grateful to my neighbors right now."

"I think you should be. Can you show me what belongs to Mr. Samuels?"

"I'd be delighted." She stood up and we started going through the apartment. It didn't take long; it was a small place. She dumped his junk in a couple of paper grocery bags. All there was, was a few pieces of clothing, some toiletries, a phone charger, a coffee grinder, and a pound of aspirational coffee beans.

I was relieved it was so little. It reinforced my sense that she was not super-involved with him. "Do you have any personal belongings at Mr. Samuels' residence?"

"No. I've never been there." She put the bags down by the door. "Tell Officer Dominguez I appreciate the help tonight."

"I'll do that. Glad we could be of assistance. These things can go bad."

"I know." She was staring at me. I wondered what she saw. "How long have you been a cop?"

"Three years." Her eyebrows went up. I knew I looked a little old. "I was in the Army for twelve years."

"Ah. Thank you for your service. My dad was in, too." She stared at me for another few seconds, or forever.

Something happened. It was like the light changed color, or the air changed temperature, or the sound of the nearly-silent building changed to soft music. I shook my head, confused. Narrowed my eyes, wondering if she'd noticed anything, but she didn't speak. "I'll take these down. You lock that door now, and take care."

"You too," she said. "Take care, Officer Kravitz."

I stepped out with the bags and waited to hear the door close, the deadbolt sink, and the chain slide. Then I went downstairs to make sure Samuels fucked off like he was supposed to. Dominguez wrote down his license-plate number, watched him go, asked me a couple of questions to clarify or confirm points we'd observed, then said, "Thanks for the backup. This was an easy one."

"A good outcome," I said. "See you back at the ranch." We nodded to each other, he got in his car, I got in mine. Gave him a minute to head out and call in before following him and doing the same. With any luck there wouldn't be anything else to respond to. From now till end of watch – about the time it began to get light – all I expected to do was pull over a few drunks or give a few warnings for jaywalking or loitering. The wee small hours of the morning, in Las Vegas. I thought about Gloria Louise pretty much the entire time.

She'd looked different, of course. On stage she wore rockabilly-style dresses, with her dark hair up in a loose way that showed off the roses tattooed around her neck and the thorny stems on her shoulders. Her eyes were outlined with black in that kind of exaggerated, Egyptian way, and her mouth was always painted red. On this night, off duty or after the show, her hair was down and she wore no makeup. I tried not to think about whether she might or might not have had anything on under that spa robe. I knew what her shape

5

was like. Full and lush, an hourglass, an armful. I hadn't been close to a shape like that for what seemed a very long time. I couldn't help thinking, there's no rule against a cop asking a piano player out for coffee. Or a drink. Or dinner. There was no arrest, so she wasn't – technically – a witness. I couldn't help wondering how she would take it if I did. If that would freak her out. I knew maybe more than she might be comfortable with, about what she might do in certain circumstances. On the other hand, I knew she had boundaries. I respected that. We all need to have boundaries, and we all deserve to have our boundaries respected.

I had never given a moment's thought to how she would act in a situation like that. It's not something that is first in mind when you're watching someone perform. I'd been impressed. For starters, I was impressed that she only hit Samuels once. From the little she said and the nothing he said, I guessed that bruise was from her elbow. I would not have minded the opportunity to intimidate that guy a little. She probably would have gotten him out of there without further trouble, but because of the neighbor's call it was a done deal, nobody was hurt, and he knew we had eyes on him. A good outcome. It was good knowing the next time I saw her I wouldn't be wondering if she was going out with him after the show. *None of your business, Kravitz*, I told myself.

She was a really good piano player. A songwriter. I'd found that show almost the minute it opened, about eighteen months ago. I grew up with Sinatra and the Rat Pack in the house all the time. My folks live in Atlantic City. My dad is an accountant for a casino, and my mother works in one of their big performance lounges. First a server, then a bartender, and now a manager. She still wears high heels and a short skirt on the job, and she still bitches about having to settle for this or that pop or country singer instead of Gino Corsetti. It just so happens Corsetti is from Atlantic City too. When I told Mom I got to see his show almost every week, she said something very rude.

I wondered what she would say if I actually got a date with Gloria Louise. Mom knew all about The Desert Rogues. Which meant my father, my sister, my brother-in-law, their three kids, and all the extended family did too. I might be very popular back in Jersey if this worked out.

And I might be getting way ahead of myself. I would give it a couple of weeks, I decided. Keep an eye on the blotter and make sure that Samuels guy didn't go back there – or show up at the casino – looking for trouble. I would go to Corsetti's show when I could. And if everything seemed cool, I'd send around an invitation for coffee, or a drink. My commander knew I liked the third watch, even though it made dating tough. But for someone else who worked nights, it wouldn't be as much of an issue. I was getting ahead of myself again. I couldn't help it. I knew I'd be listening to that album when I got home. Gino Corsetti and The Desert Rogues: What If It Were True.

Corsetti got married in April. When he sang that title song, he always dedicated it to his husband. I didn't know many out gay guys – the Army still favors don't ask, don't tell, and the cop shop did too – but I could respect the guy for guts, and for commitment. I had a feeling Gloria Louise would not be okay with dating someone who was not okay with Corsetti. I had a feeling I was going to be okay with anything she wanted.

I - Gloria

September 2015

I told Gino and the Rogues about the whole police incident. Not exactly why, just that it happened. I might not have if Gino hadn't given me a long frowning look in the green room the next day and said, "What's the matter?" Of course I tried to play it off, but he knew me pretty well by then. "Give his picture to casino security," he said. "Tell them he's not welcome."

"I don't have a restraining order," I said. It was a weak objection and I knew it. Gino gave me his very most Chairman of the Don't Fuck With Me expression. It was pretty effective considering he doesn't have a mean bone in his body. "Okay, yes, I will." He nodded, and we moved on to choosing our set for the night. Ruben and Oscar, our drums and bass, didn't really say anything, but they made sure I never walked out alone after the show anymore. I wanted to be annoyed about it, but it was too nice being cared for. Looked after. It had been a long time since I had that.

I was thirty-five and finally – by my own standards – successful. Our show at the casino packed them in, and our first record together was doing well. That was mostly Sinatra-esque covers of standards, but Gino did a few of my songs too, and one of them was the title track. I'd kind of loved him from the very start – it's hard not to love someone who picks you out of half-a-dozen piano players and says 'she's perfect' – but I really loved him after that. I loved Ruben and Oscar too, partly because they always seemed sincerely cool with me running the trio. That was unique in my experience, and I was certain it was due to the fact that

Gino chose me first. And then had me sit with him while he auditioned all the people who came in for bass and drums. It was, basically, a dream job. The only problem with it was the whole working six nights a week thing. My schedule was incompatible with those of most acceptably-employed single men. Consequently, I tended to find dates among other casino employees, which was where I found that fucker Travis Samuels.

Two weeks after the police incident, I spotted the cop in the audience. Not the Latino guy, who'd seemed a little too ready to do that thing so many men do. Not exactly blaming the victim, not saying you deserved it or you asked for it, maybe more implying I contributed to creating a situation where a guy thinks he can make me do something. And the sad part is I get that. From one point of view, I did exactly that. I had sex with a man and I gave him a key to my apartment, and those two things add up to 'well that means he has rights over you' for a whole hell of a lot of people. But the thing is, it doesn't mean that. Just because I had sex with him once, he didn't have the right to have sex with me again. It was and is my choice, every single time. And this other cop, the one who was in the Army for a while and still looked like he could command a boot camp, the one who was tall and broad enough to make me feel petite and yet whose presence in my apartment had been not a threat but a comfort, the one I now remembered seeing here more than once before ... that cop clearly understood boundaries. He'd been pissed when the other officer asked that question, and when he'd asked about my robe.

He was out there in a sport jacket that might have been gray or blue, cut well enough to minimize his size, at a non-gaming table. He had a drink in front of him. Officer Kravitz. I wondered what his first name was.

During the mid-set break I told Gino, "The good cop is here."

His eyebrows went up. "Did you know he was coming?"

"Nope."

"Do you mind?"

"Nope." I almost stopped with that. Then, because this was Gino, "He's been here before. He knew who I was, when they came to the apartment. I didn't invite him to come back. Here, I mean."

"I'm sure he didn't expect you to." Gino sounded slightly amused. I think he thought I am more irresistible to men than I actually am. I am very resistible, apparently. Which, now that I thought about it, made the cop's presence here best described as gratifying. He'd seen me at my worst, after all. I wasn't saying anything. After a moment Gino nudged me and said, "You want to swap anything in to the second half?"

And I realized I did. "Could we do 'My Time of Day?' You don't do that much but it's legit Sinatra." All the tunes – well, all the guy tunes – from 'Guys and Dolls' get a workout with us.

"What do you think, fellas? Can we fake it well enough?"

"I can fake it like a debutante," said Ruben, whose knowledge of debutantes all came from the movie 'Gone with the Wind' as far as I knew. Maybe there was some debutante porn out there I didn't know about. At any rate, Gino didn't pursue that. We all flipped to the number in our fake books – that's a thing when you have to be ready to perform a few hundred songs; it's like a page for each song, with the chords and the basic structure, enough to get you through if you dry up – and then went back out onstage.

Kravitz was still there. I tried to be subtle, pointing him out to Gino. Then he completely blew my cover when, after three songs, he said, "Here's a number we like to do from time to time. It's going out to everybody who lives at night like we do, including a friend of ours from the LVPD. 'My Time of Day,' folks." I wanted to kill him, but I played the intro, resolutely looking only at what was happening on stage. The reason that song wasn't in regular rotation was, it's tricky. It's not danceable. It hasn't got a conventional pop structure. It says more about the character of Sky Masterson than the whole rest of the musical, really. Anyway Gino sang the hell out of it as usual, and when he finished I couldn't resist checking in with Kravitz. He was watching me. I almost smiled. He almost smiled. Then a server was there. Kravitz looked up and said something to him, and I suddenly remembered the way Gino's husband Sergei got the ball rolling for them, and I squealed a little on the inside.

I am not a girl who squeals, even on the inside. It was so surprising, so disorienting, I had to mentally shake myself and focus on the rest of the set. I did not look out at the audience. I did my best to play off Ruben and Oscar and Gino, who wrapped up the night with Sinatra's classic 'Put Your Dreams Away.' Then we took our bows, the stage lights shut down, and we headed off. Imagine my surprise to find that server waiting to give me a message. Would I meet Mr. Kravitz in the piano bar for a drink? Yes, yes I would. I gave Alberto a fiver and watched him go. Then I turned to see Ruben, Oscar, and Gino all grinning at me. "Shut up," I said. They made identical 'we didn't say anything' faces. We all trooped into the green room. I checked myself out in the mirror, thinking I looked acceptable, glad I didn't have to carry a purse or other bullshit. This is why I have my dresses made with pockets. Two good-sized pockets in a full skirt with a crinoline can accommodate a lot of crap. Cigarettes, lighter, Listerine strips, and keys in one; lipstick, phone, access card, and a Mighty Wallet in the other. Hands-free operation.

I was tempted to pause for a smoke before going over to the piano bar. That was a holdover from the days I used to smoke more. The truth is, I'm down to one cigarette a day, before we play. On our days off I have that smoke around the same time. I knew it was bad for me, and I really didn't even crave it anymore. It was ceremonial. Gino usually came out with me. He hadn't smoked in twenty years – he was taking better care of his instrument than Sinatra himself had, and it showed – but he liked the way it smelled. And it was a moment for the two of us alone. We didn't talk all that much, but when we had something to confide, we did it then. It occurred to me I didn't have to smoke during that moment. Maybe it was time to quit for good. If Kravitz didn't smoke, maybe I'd quit.

Decision made, I popped a Listerine strip in my mouth and swished it around while I freshened up my lipstick. Then I said "See you tomorrow" to the guys and strolled away.

He was standing by the bar, waiting for me. He didn't have a drink yet. Even with my heels on, he was taller than me. "Ms. Bartolo."

"Call me Gloria." I stuck out my hand. He gravely shook it. I let go and said, "What's your name?"

"Call me Lou," he said. "Can I buy you a drink?"

12

"Well, of course you can." He might not have known those were two lines from a song. "Whisky on the rocks, please." I smiled and went past him, not to a barstool but to a low two-top in the corner. At this hour there actually was no piano player, so what I heard was piped in. "I was going to a different piano bar for a while," I said, making conversation as Lou joined me. "This Argentine guy plays every summer, down the Strip. That's where I met Travis." Putting that right out there.

It didn't faze him. "Have you heard from him?"

"Nope."

"Good." He looked as though he was crossing something off a mental list.

I smiled again. "Were you always going to invite me for a drink, or was it because we played that song?"

Now he smiled. It occurred to me this was the first time I'd seen that. It was well worth waiting for; his Strong Silent Serious face relaxed, and I could see how the lines on that face, lines burned in from days in the sun, fit into the smile. He said, "I was always going to invite you. It was tonight because you played that song."

"You've been here before. Tell me about you and music." It was a gamble, but I thought he wouldn't have been coming only to see me. And I was right. He told me about his parents, and their casino jobs back East, and about the music he grew up with. I told him about being an Army brat, and discovering standards and show tunes because of a junior-high band teacher. He asked when I started writing songs. "Immediately," I said, and he laughed. He had a good laugh, too. "They were garbage at first."

"We all have to start somewhere."

I wanted to know where he started. Why the Army, why leave it, why become a cop. But I thought that might get heavy, and I didn't want to, not tonight. I also didn't want to stay out too late, and I wasn't ready to invite him back to my place. We'd been talking for almost two hours. He got to the end of a college story – he'd gone to a public university in New Jersey, I'd gone to a community college in New Mexico – and glanced at his watch. "Yeah," I said. "Me too. I'd like to see you again, Lou Kravitz."

"I'd like to see you again, Gloria Louise. When could that happen?" We exchanged numbers and consulted calendars. My schedule was upside down, but it was regular. His was going to be less regular. He apologized for that.

"Don't apologize," I said. "If it's worth doing, we'll find a way to do it."

That seemed to amuse him. "That's generally how it works, isn't it? I'll call you if Wednesday stays free. That good?"

"That's great." I watched him wonder if he should try for a kiss. "Thanks for the drink." I leaned over and kissed him lightly. He was smiling when I walked away.

I didn't have an agenda for what happened next, believe it or not. This was not the first time a cop, or a military guy, or an athlete, had shown non-professional interest in me. I was clearly not an athlete; I was a big girl with an attitude, and that appeals to a certain kind of man. The kind who doesn't want to have to try to minimize his own size, or to handle someone with kid gloves all the time. I didn't try to be cute. I didn't try to be thin. I wasn't built for that, and I'd long ago found a size and a number that worked for me in terms of energy and health, and whoever thought that size or that number were too big or too high could go fuck himself. Anyone who thought I should get a normal job, a day job, so I could be 'available' at normal hours could also go fuck himself.

Whereas anyone who came to the show I worked on – it was tempting to say 'my show' but, you know, Gino – and looked at me as if I were the star, and said he'd like to see me again, and didn't try to talk me into more than the drink I'd agreed to … that person had my interest. I had a pretty good bullshit detector. If I saw Officer Kravitz a few more times and I was not detecting anything other than the equivalent interest (and by 'equivalent' I mean 'sexually focused but respectful') there was a good chance this whole thing could get very much more interesting.

II - Lou

October 2015

It's hard to put a value on connections. Some don't seem all that important, and you find out later those are the people who will save your life. Others seem completely essential, until one day you look around and wonder why you bothered. I wasn't sure where to rank Gloria. I didn't see her very often, and when I did, nothing much happened. It was always after a show. She didn't kiss me again. I wasn't inclined to push for anything, because of the way we met. I couldn't tell if she was waiting to be asked for more, or if she was taking her time making up her mind.

I was used to waiting; it didn't bother me. I was used to being disappointed, too. I'm well aware some people – not only women – find me scary. I'm tall, I'm an athlete, I've got enough nose for two people, and my hair is going, at least on my head. My eyebrows are another story. The blue eyes that looked kind of soft and dreamy twenty years ago were now surrounded by lines that I knew aged me. Plus they added up to 'suspicion' or even 'hostility.' Too many days squinting during maneuvers in the sun. Nothing I could do to offset that except speak softly and move lightly. Nobody expected that from someone my size.

Gloria wasn't scared of me. That, I was sure of. She liked me, too, or she wouldn't have been meeting up with me as often as she did, even if it didn't feel like 'often.' She wouldn't have stopped smoking, either. I didn't ask her to. I didn't even mention it. She volunteered the information, the fourth time we met up after the show. Then she sat there, tapping her glass with those short black-lacquered nails, waiting for me to comment.

"How long did you smoke?" I asked after a minute.

"Since I was fourteen. Twenty-one years."

That amused me, the oblique way of telling me how old she was. Neither of us had specified, though I was fairly sure she'd estimated my age from all the numbers I'd given her. Three years on the force, twelve years in the service, four years of college: she could do the math. "A lot of my high-school friends smoked," I said. "My mom too, for a long time. Then her mother got lung cancer and they both quit. Dad had this cleaning service come in and basically wash the house. The water was disgusting."

"God, I know!" She made a face. "I haven't smoked indoors for a long time, because this one time in college? I went to see a rental house, and the person who lived there before was a chain smoker. There were tar stains on everything. The ceiling, the walls, the fucking vertical blinds, all this gross orange color and the place reeked. I was like, no."

I laughed. "So why did you stop." It was none of my business, really, but I thought she wouldn't have mentioned it at all if she didn't want to tell me why. "Did your boss ask you to?"

"Gino? No. He kind of liked it. My one smoke a day, before the show, with him. It was a nostalgia trip for him."

"So what did he say?"

"He said, what do you put in that pocket now." She watched me laugh. "I told him I got a deck of cards and he said do not gamble, and I said I never gamble. Which of course was a lie."

"What's your game?" She didn't really seem like a gambler. I never played, myself. When people asked why, I told them I liked to waste my money on tangible things. She didn't answer for a minute. The pause had a quality of 'how much should I say.' I didn't push, only waited.

"I have gambled on men," she said, finally. "As you know." I nodded. Then she swerved. "Would you say the way I present myself invites a certain degree of fuckery?"

I must have looked astonished; she laughed. I said, "Fuck no," while she was still laughing. She took a mouthful of whisky, then set the glass down again with her eyebrows up like 'please proceed.' I watched her throat move as she swallowed. She noticed, of course. Her eyes narrowed a bit as if she were suppressing something. I hoped it was a smile. I said, "In my opinion, which you have solicited –"

"Yes, I have."

"The way you present yourself does three things. It suits your profession, as you look both theatrical and professional. It tells people you're a planner, a person who does things intentionally. And it suits your particular beauty perfectly." Her mouth literally fell open. I couldn't remember ever having that effect on a woman before. On a man, yes, a junior platoon member who didn't expect to have his ass handed to him by me. I waited for her to speak. Did I mention I'm used to waiting?

"You think I'm beautiful?" She was staring at me as if this was the sixty-four-thousand-dollar question, which I guess it was.

"Of course I do," I said after a nanosecond to ask myself if I wanted to lay it all out there. Obviously the answer was 'yes,' or else my mouth got ahead of my brain. "You've got great legs, great tits, great hair, great skin, the mouth of an angel and the eyes of a devil. I think you're gorgeous." It seemed I had rendered her speechless. "Do people not tell you this?"

"No," she said finally. "Once in a while they mention my tits." I laughed. She drank the rest of her whisky so quickly I winced. Then she stood up and held out her hand. I took it and stood up myself. "Let's go for a walk," she said. I'd already paid for our drinks, so I followed her out. At first I thought 'walk' might be a euphemism, but it wasn't. She was wearing heels, the vintage-looking saddle shoes she always wore on stage. I don't know how comfortable those were to walk in, but she moved easily. And she didn't let go of my hand. It was a good ten minutes before she said anything else. It was the middle of the night and none too warm outside. She finally stopped at that fence where you can watch the fountain at Bellagio. "Put your arm around me." I did that. "Thanks."

"You're welcome." Using me for a windbreak. I was okay with that. It was the first time I'd touched more than her hand. She was snug against my side. Of course my cock immediately told me I was holding a woman. I stared at the fountain. My cock said something about how long it had been since the last time I held a woman. I bit the inside of my lip. It was ridiculous to be this turned on by such an innocuous contact. I breathed slowly through my nose and tried to think about unsexy things.

"What did you study in college?" The question came out of nowhere.

I wasn't sure why she asked, but it didn't really matter. "History. You?"

"Music." Another minute passed. "Why history? That doomed to repeat it thing?"

"I knew I wanted to serve. With a degree and the reserve officers training program, I had a shot at a

19

commission. I don't like math." That was a lie, but it sounded true. She laughed under her breath. I turned toward her, not completely, maybe forty-five degrees. Geometry has a lot of applications. She looked up at me. "May I kiss you?"

"Yes, you may."

So I kissed her, and my cock instantly woke way the hell up, because her mouth was perfect and it opened right away. She tasted of whisky. She slid her arms around me and pressed close. I could feel her smile and I knew she was feeling my erection. It was a long time, but nowhere near long enough, before she stepped back. Not out of my arms, only enough to put some space between us so we could breathe. I needed to. "Gloria."

She looked so luscious. Sleepy-eyed, a little flushed. "Well, that answers one question. Actually two."

"Which two questions would those be?"

"Whether I would like kissing you, and whether you would like kissing me."

"Who wouldn't like kissing you?" My tone was incredulous.

"You'd be surprised." Her tone was dry. "For the record, I like kissing you."

"Good. Can we do some more of that?"

She smiled, and ran her thumb under my bottom lip. I hadn't noticed her hand leaving my body. The other one was still there. "Walk me back to my car." That was not a 'yes' but it was also not a 'no.' I kept my arm around her and we strolled back the way we came. My cock was strenuously objecting to my failure to progress from that hot wet mouth to another hot wet aperture. I was strongly hoping I would get the chance

20

soon, if not tonight. I wanted to see and feel her entire body. I wanted all of her in my mouth. I wanted to make her come, screaming, and then … *Jesus*. I turned my attention to the Strip, counting taxis, watching for patrol cars, looking for anything to keep my mind off all this delicious woman. Back to the casino, inside, walking through without speaking. She led me through the green room and down a nondescript corridor, and out a back door. Then across the parking lot to her car. When we got there she leaned against it, shifting from one foot to the other. "That was a longer walk than I bargained for."

"I could rub your feet for you."

Her face actually lit up, and she laughed. "I'll bet you could. Not tonight. But soon."

I was about to ask if I could kiss her again when she saved me the trouble by kissing me. When she finally tore her mouth out from under mine I had her pressed up against her car – a red Mazda compact SUV – and I was about one more move from coming in my pants. "Jesus," I said, breathless. "I'm sorry." I moved my feet back, opening up some space.

"Mmm." She had her hands on my hips. She stroked up with her thumbs, skimming over my shirt, going for the bottom of my rib cage. I could feel the moment when she discovered that scar. "What happened here?"

"Iraq."

"How many others?"

"You'll have to count them for yourself."

She was smiling. "The next time I see you. Dinner. And then we'll continue this conversation. If you want to."

I leaned in again, let my hard cock press against her. "What do you think?"

"I think you want to." She still had her hands on me. She brushed one of them up between the lapels of my sport coat, all the way up to my throat, and around the back of my neck. Then she brought it forward, curling her fingers, brushing her knuckles across the side of my face and her thumb across my mouth. "I'll text you."

"Mmm." It was all I could manage. She let go of me; I stepped away. She got in the car and I watched her drive out of the parking lot. After a minute I collected myself enough to look around. I had no idea how to get back to where I left my motorcycle. I walked in the direction she'd taken. Once I was on a street I'd know where the hell I was.

I still might not be sure I knew what the hell I was doing. What she was doing. What we were doing. God, I liked her so much. I really hoped this was going somewhere.

II - Gloria

October 2015

That walk and those kisses were on a Wednesday. Which meant four days till my next day off, and I had no idea if Lou would have to work on Sunday night, or on Monday. As soon as I got home I sent a text: *I'm off Sunday 23:00 to Tuesday 17:00. You?*

His answer came back fast. I wondered if he was at home yet, or if he was sitting in his car, or if he was walking from the employee parking area to wherever he'd left his car. I had no idea where he lived or what he drove. That was the first time we'd left the casino. His reply read: *I'll see if I can swap a shift. Let you know ASAP*

Great. Btw nice mouth

LOL you too

Looking forward to getting acquainted with the rest of you

Stop it. He added a smiley face. God, I liked him so much. I wanted to fuck him till I couldn't walk. I wanted to fuck him till *he* couldn't walk. I wondered what he would look like naked. If he was hairy, if he was tanned all over. His forearms were tanned. I'd noticed that our first time in the piano bar. The AC was wonky and it was warm. He took off his sport coat and rolled up his sleeves. No tattoos showing there at least, and no jewelry on those big square hands. I hadn't fucked a white guy for a long time. I wondered if he was circumcised. Kravitz was, I thought, a Jewish name. We hadn't talked about religion. Maybe he guessed that my religion was music. All I'd gotten from him was a refreshing distaste for patriarchy. I bet I would love his mother.

Stop it, I told myself. *One step at a time*. My panties were soaked and the insides of my thighs were sticky. I wondered if he could tell he got me off, rubbing against me that way outside my car. I'd made some kind of sound but he was not quite all there in that moment. I thought he would have gone too in a few more seconds. He'd stopped himself. A man with control.

I got undressed, checked my crinoline to see if I needed to sponge it out, did that. Took off my makeup, took down my hair. I was kind of hungry now that I wasn't distracted by Officer Big Cock. I threw on that spa robe, the one that actually was stolen, though not by me. Gino called it a souvenir from when he lived in the casino hotel, before moving in with Sergei. That had happened less than two months after they met. I was thinking about what Gino told me while I made myself a grilled cheese sandwich. He said after a month of talking and a week of perfect nights, they didn't have any questions left except the ones that could only be answered by living together.

I couldn't help wondering if Lou was open to living with a piano player.

I ate my sandwich standing up, licked my fingers, wiped out the nonstick frying pan, and went to stretch. That was a thing I did now because of Gino, who did it because of Sergei. Sergei, who used to be a professional dancer and who now trained showgirls. He was great. Five or six years older than Gino, tough as nails, a Russian-American Jew from New York. A man who loved my boss so much you could see it around them like an aura. To call what I felt about the pair of them 'envy' was very fair. There was some fear, too, because when they met Gino was forty-seven, and the thought of waiting that long to find my true love was scary.

I could tell myself I didn't need that, that I was fine. Alone was good because I could play or write whenever I wanted. I didn't have to account for myself, or my whack schedule, or the days I wanted to spend at Gino and Sergei's, to anybody. It was all bullshit. I wanted a man. A partner, a lover, maybe even – if this was possible given I was not ever going to change jobs by choice – a husband. Who would put up with me? Me and my job and my compulsive need to make music. There honestly had been no one. No one stuck. I was a little too tall for most men, a little too heavy, a little too … the way I was. No one had called me beautiful since my Samoan grandma died.

Until tonight.

Your particular beauty, he said. I think you're gorgeous, he said. And then he asked if he could kiss me, instead of assuming, and when I stopped he stopped. If he didn't fuck as perfectly as he did everything else I was going to throw myself off the Hoover Dam.

Of course I wasn't. I am not that girl. I was a little worked up, that's all. I wanted to bang on a piano, and all I have at home is a digital. It has weighted keys, it's a great instrument, but it was not the big solid acoustic at Gino and Sergei's house, the one Gino had me choose. He was going to be thrilled if this thing with Lou worked out. My boss, my friend, my confidante. I knew I'd be telling him everything tomorrow. Or, more accurately, later today. It was time for bed.

I did not sleep all that well, but I applied some discipline and got out of bed when my alarm went off. Dragged myself to the shitty little gym in my building and spent a half hour on the treadmill, then went back upstairs to stretch, shower, and make breakfast. After cleaning that up I spent an hour at the keyboard. I was working on some new material, because Gino wanted to do another album. We still had some buzz from 'What If It Were True,' and now we were getting a little more buzz because of a book. At first it was a series of articles in one of the local papers, about Las Vegas performers. USA Today picked that up, and then the writer got a book deal. She'd talked to Gino and Sergei, and they got friendly, and it seemed like anytime any of them had an interview they always talked about each other.

I should clarify. Sergei didn't really talk to the media. The world knew he and Gino were married, but Sergei had been off the stage for over a decade. His role in the showgirl extravaganza was completely behind the scenes. He also – according to Gino – got a kick out of The Desert Rogues and any little moments of attention we got. Gino confided that Sergei had some nerves about our show. Not that he thought there was anything wrong with it, but he was afraid it wouldn't be enough for Gino, who lived on the road for twenty-five years. So the more successful we got, the more secure Sergei felt, and I could definitely sympathize with that. I was a homebody myself. I would have gone on tour with Gino if I had to. Not going on tour suited me fine.

Anyway, I was working up this song cycle. After going-on-two-years playing together, I knew Gino's voice and how he liked to sing, and also what he could do that didn't make it to the casino stage very often. He's a good singer, is what I'm saying, and the fact that he *could* sound exactly like Frank Sinatra did not mean he couldn't do anything else. This song cycle was for a concept album about a guy who comes to Vegas and hits it big, runs into trouble, but manages to fix it. A fairy tale, if I didn't know a few people with that actual story. There would be up-tempo numbers and a couple of boozy ballads, a fight song and a love song (or two). I really couldn't wait to hand it all over to the guys and see what they said. It is a hell of a thing to have people of talent say 'we can't wait to hear what you do next,' and to then take it and make it better, and to do that without picking it apart and changing it. I had one previous collaboration experience, which ended in screaming. This was not that. I had to set an alarm because otherwise I would lose track of time.

A lot of songs start – for me – with a simple premise. Like: I want to write a ballad that sounds like something Sinatra would have done in the Forties. Something Irving Berlin or Cole Porter or the Gershwins might have written. I've been listening to and playing that stuff for a quarter of a century and I studied songwriting in college, so I'm not pulling it out of a hat. Once I have the premise, it typically takes one or two hours to write the lyric, and by the time I have the lyric I can generally hear the melody. This concept project was a little different because the whole album needed to tell a cohesive story. Every song could not sound the same. I wanted the overall impression to be one of energy. Ambition, hope, persistence, cussedness. The hero of this story kept trying, even if his strategy was crap for a while. And he learned. He changed. He evolved, so he could earn his happy ending. I guess this came from a lot of years reading romance novels. Nobody wants a hero who doesn't have to work for it. God, this was fun.

My alarm buzzed. I swore at it, finished the note I was making, and switched off the keyboard. Hung up my headphones and went to get dressed for work. Only when I was doing that did I wonder what Lou Kravitz was doing today. I told myself severely not to wonder what he did last night after I left. It was none of my business if he got himself off at home, or if he thought of me while he did that.

I wondered anyway. I was laughing at myself when I got to the casino. Gino took one look at me and said, "Good date?"

"Very good date," I said. "We're going out to dinner Monday if he can swap a shift."

Oscar gave me a sideways smile. "Ever dated a cop before?" He was married to a police officer.

"No. Got any advice for me?"

"Well you might not do this anyway seeing how he's the size of a bus. But Lorena had to tell me, like a million times, don't fuss. She says yes it can be dangerous but it usually isn't so shut up and let me get on with it."

I would never admit that I'd already had those thoughts. Being big and strong didn't necessarily mean much in a world full of guns. For no reason I said, "Lou was in the Army for twelve years. I know he got hurt while he was in."

Oscar nodded. "With any luck he's done with that." Ruben and Gino made supportive noises, and we got our books out to plan the set. Gino told me that writer asked why we didn't play the same set every time. He said he looked at her like she was crazy, wondering if she was serious, until she cracked up laughing and said but readers will ask! Some of them just won't get it! They'll be all, but that's so much work. And it was, but that's why *we* had this gig instead of somebody else. The ability to play (and sing) a hundred years' worth of great pop songs did not grow on trees. Gino was a musician in his bones. I still had moments when I couldn't believe he wanted to work with me. We did a little warmup there in the green room, skipped through a couple of songs that were relatively new to the slate, and then it was time to go on. I still couldn't believe that either, sometimes.

The lounge was packed, as usual these days, and we were hot. The first half went great, and I'd almost forgotten about the whole cop thing until I turned on my phone during the break and found a text: *Mission accomplished. Off duty Sunday 20:00 to Tuesday 15:00*

I texted back fast: *Meet me here post show?*

His reply: *Yes ma'am.* And so my concentration was shot, because it was only three more nights, and then we would have more than thirty-six hours to see if the month of talking meant something real, or if we were going to bang each other and move on.

I hadn't really cared for so long. Hadn't really tried. Hadn't examined the random tolerable man in front of me and asked myself if this was more than scratching an itch. I did not screw up the set, let me be clear. However I also did not, after the fact, really remember playing the rest of it. Half of my brain was occupied with the horrifying realization that I wanted a lot from Lou. A lot more than I'd wanted before, ever, from anyone.

And I hadn't even fucked him yet.

III - Lou

October 2015

I probably don't need to mention what I did as soon as I got home from that walk with Gloria, or what I did the next day in the shower before going in to work. It was a good thing the criminals of Las Vegas were feeling unambitious, I guess; I cannot deny I was a little distracted. I stood my watch, did my patrols, gave warnings and move-alongs and tickets; checked in with a few local businesses that we kept an eye on; and generally did the job.

I imagined, going into the academy, that police work would be the way it was on TV: all action, all the time. I should have known better. After all, military life was not much like the way it looked in the movies. With the reporting we had to do on everything, a typical shift didn't seem to produce much value. But if you've been places where 'public safety' has no meaning beyond 'did my family and I live through the day,' you see why it's worth doing. There is value to the law-abiding driver in knowing that the speeder, the tail-gater, the red-light-runner will eventually get caught. There is value to the small business owner in knowing that the cops will hassle those hooligans on the corner and make the block safe for customers. Obviously, if you're the hooligan or the red-light-runner, you bitch about the police state and yap about infringement of personal liberty.

I let the bitching and yapping slide off most of the time. Some of those people talked themselves into more serious citations, or bigger fines. I was the cop who would let an idiot keep blowing up until I was justified taking them to jail. It didn't take me long to discover that some people really never had faced the consequences of their antisocial behavior. A few hours in a holding cell could be very educational. In two years I'd done that with eight misdemeanor calls, and seven of those people did not get in trouble again. We didn't always pursue charges if we got a promise to get anger management or substance abuse or whatever kind of counseling. We told people that was much cheaper and easier than losing your job because you now had an arrest record.

The department was willing to deal with the lower arrest rate – and this was a trivial skim off the top of that, even though I was not the only cop who did it – if it meant a higher proportion of arraignments involved people who were actually a menace to society. Your average asshole is not going to hold up a liquor store. He (or she) also doesn't want to be sitting on a bench across from the kind of person who really will hold up a liquor store. Most average assholes have never looked a real criminal in the face. Most of them don't want to do it more than once.

I knew Gloria wondered why I became a cop. Why I didn't stay in the Army. I had a couple of promotions under my belt and could certainly have stayed in for twenty years, even after the last injury. I could have retired as a lieutenant colonel, and then done whatever. One day I guessed we would talk about that. For now I was content to be on a different front line. I discouraged my fellow officers from calling me Captain, because that wasn't my police rank and probably never would be. I didn't have a sense that this was going to be my last job, that I'd found the real me. I didn't tell people that, thanks to a few really good nights at the casino when I was in college, and thanks to having invested every after-tax penny, and thanks to not having school debt or kids or a divorce, I didn't really need to worry about job security.

Everyone I knew who was around my age had some degree of money trouble. Most of the time it was minor, and transient. Sometimes it was serious and systemic. A gambling town has a lot of potential pitfalls. When I told my parents I was going to settle in Las Vegas instead of Jersey, they thought I was crazy. Dad asked me straight out, are you going to gamble. He didn't approve, even though he knew I stopped after that big year. I said no, it's the landscape I like. There's something restful to me in that inhospitable emptiness. The desert doesn't care if you live or die. The East Coast is too easy. And it has too many people. I like being able to see the horizon.

I found a fifty-year-old ranch house, a little bit far out of town. I suspected the town might reach out to it one day, so I spent a little extra to buy land around the house. I had twelve acres, enough to sell off a bit if I wanted to, and if the price was right. The house needed a lot of work. I had pretty good handyman skills but I didn't want the rehab to take ten years. So I kept an eye out for someone who'd make a good roommate. Someone with skills, more interested in making something than in chasing girls or cards or booze. I did not expect to find the guy outside the police station.

When I saw him, I thought he was there to make a report. He was wearing a clean pair of jeans, work boots, a plaid flannel shirt, and a baseball cap. He went in ahead of me, and because I liked his looks (maybe it was the full mustache with its waxed ends curled) I halfway listened, and heard him say something about impound. The next thing I knew I was helping him reclaim his truck, which had been stolen from a worksite with all his tools inside. He was a carpenter. His name was Ignacio González. He was five years older than me, eight inches shorter, unmarried, a licensed contractor, and an absolute nut. He told me to call him Gonzo. I visited a couple of his jobs (it's easy to check up on people, when you're a cop) and we had a couple of meals together. A couple of beers later, he told me he was saving up to get married. His inamorata ran La Cholla, the Mexican restaurant we were sitting in. He introduced us. She looked me over and seemed to think I might be a good influence, or at least a good connection. She sent me home with a tub of enchiladas and an idea.

A couple weeks later I tracked him down again and told him my idea. During the interim I ran a background check, because there are some charming criminals out there, but he came up clean. I told him I did that and he said he would have done the same. Anyway, the point of the story is Gonzo came to live out at the ranch house, and instead of paying rent he worked on stuff when he had the time. The biggest thing was tearing down a shitty unpermitted addition and re-doing it properly. The house was thirty percent bigger now, three bedrooms and 2.5 baths, all legal, and within sight of being fully habitable. It was shaped like an F. The two wings extending back into the desert formed a courtyard. In a couple of months the budget would allow for doing a pergola-type roof over the courtyard. Not a full enclosure, only planks set at an angle to keep off the worst of the sun so it could be a useful outdoor space.

Some of the interior was still unfinished. I mean, it was open studs. I was determined not to borrow for this, or to dip into my savings, so I was letting it take as long as it took now that the roof was on. That was a big-ticket item, built from structural insulated panels and covered with photovoltaic shingles. Gonzo didn't seem to find anything odd about my approach. He didn't complain about the commute, and he could be relied on to bring home food from Salma's restaurant a few times a week. We got along great. I wondered what Gloria would make of the whole situation. When it started, I was dating someone, and that woman didn't like it. She didn't like the house, or the distance from town, or my motorcycle, or Gonzo. Before long I knew I liked all those things more than I liked her.

I found myself hoping pretty strongly that Gloria would be as different from the last girl in that way as she was in every other way. I hoped she would look at the yet-unfinished house and see something she could put her mark on. I hoped she would see that extra bedroom, looking out to the desert on two sides and the courtyard on the third, and think 'that's perfect for a piano.'

And I hadn't even taken her to bed yet. I wondered what a good length of time was between one and the other. From the first night together to taking her to see my house. I literally had no idea, and asking my mother was not super helpful at first. She said, "Your house isn't even finished. Do not take her out there."

"Mom, come on."

"Are you out of your mind? A woman likes a man who finishes things."

"I *am* finishing it!"

"You're taking forever!"

"You and Dad told me not to borrow!" This was a very typical conversation. I was halfway to cracking up even though I was exasperated.

"Are we going to like this girl?"

Oh, crap. I knew that was coming. If I told Mom who it was she was not going to give me a moment's peace until we were married, and if I didn't get Gloria to the altar I would never hear the end of it. "Mom, it's not that serious." I stopped myself a nanosecond before adding 'yet.'

"Bullshit," she said. "You're asking me when you should show a woman this house you love."

She had a point. "It's really early days," I said, like a warning.

"Louis Emmanuel Kravitz."

When she used my full name I was toast. I sighed. "It's Gloria Louise."

Dead silence for ten seconds. Then, "Gino Corsetti's Gloria Louise?" Her voice squeaked a little at the end.

"Yes, Mom."

"How much do you need to finish the walls?"

"Mom! That is not –"

"Shut up! How much?"

I knew almost to the penny, of course, even after halfway-deciding on soundproofing the third bedroom's interior wall. I also knew if I told Gonzo I needed the interior finished in two weeks (or whatever) he would drop everything else. And I knew if I gave Mom a number that sounded too low she would go to my uncle, her brother, also a contractor, and ask him if it was bullshit. So I gave her a number that was as low as I thought I could get away with (in every sense), listened to some loud, full-hearted bitching about how sneaky I was (which I thought was very unjust, though I didn't say so), waited for her to take a breath, and said, "I love you, Mom. Gotta go. I'll talk to you soon." I disconnected before she could start up again.

Then I went out to the garage to do a little inventory, and ended up spending three hours re-organizing all the stock we had stashed in there. When the cash infusion arrived, Gonzo and I could hit the ground running. I will admit, I felt better about potentially inviting Gloria to see the place if we couldn't see through any walls when she got there.

III – Gloria

October 2015

That was the longest three days of my life, which was so ridiculous I kept razzing myself about it. I got a ton of work done on the new songs, because if I wasn't fully occupied my brain went off in unproductive directions. It was worse than being sixteen again. I was fantasizing. I was next-best-thing to writing 'Gloria Louise Kravitz' in my notebook.

Gino could tell something was up. On Sunday, between sets, we went out to the parking lot for our usual private moment. He told me about the latest from the writer, the one who did those newspaper stories and that book. "Kathy doesn't know what hit her," he said. "A minute ago she was trying to get pieces on Curbed or whatever and now the Los Angeles Times is calling for comment on some backstage brouhaha there."

"She's the backstage-life expert now, huh?" I was fidgeting a little, missing the cigarette business because at least it gave me something to do with my hands. "L.A. doesn't have one already?" Gino laughed. I broke. "Were you nervous before that first date with Sergei?"

He knew I meant the first real one. When they went to dinner, after a month of conversation, knowing that after dinner they'd go to bed. "Hell yeah I was nervous. We only kissed once before then. It was a great kiss, but what if we didn't like each other in bed?" He was turned slightly toward me, and even though he seemed to be looking past me I knew he was observing my body language.

I tried not to fidget. "When did you feel like, okay, this is going to work? As soon as you got in the house?"

He snorted a little and gave the tiniest shake of his head. "I liked the house. He had cognac for me, a new bottle. I liked his cat. He showed me this guest bath that was all set up, had everything I needed. He told me he hadn't brought anyone home before."

I hadn't heard all of this before. I'd heard about the first kiss, and about the dinner, and about how the first night together was as perfect as everything else had been. "Did you ask why?"

"No." Gino was looking straight at me now. "All that mattered was that he wanted me there. And then." He stopped, and his eyes went soft. God, how he loved Sergei. "The second I put my hands on him I knew."

Oh shit. I gulped a little. One week after that, Sergei asked Gino to move in. As far as I knew, neither of them had regretted leveling up so fast. They'd both told me the only reason they waited a year to get married was so their wedding anniversary was the same day of the same month as their first meeting. So even if they were together the rest of their lives, until they were so old they couldn't remember where they were, they wouldn't forget when it started. For some reason that led me to "If I count from the first time I met Lou we've known each other for less than seven weeks."

"Plenty of time," Gino said. "If you didn't like him you wouldn't have gone for that first drink. And if you didn't want to fuck him you would have known after you kissed him."

I cast my eyes up at the hazily-dark sky. It was chilly outside, and almost time to go in again. "I have this girl thing about how someone's fuckability should not be a criterion. That all these practical metrics are more important. Is that a girl thing?"

"That is not a girl thing. Practical metrics are important. But if you're talking about potentially having a life together, fuckability is *extremely* important," Gino said gravely. I was pretty sure he was trying not to completely crack up.

"I mean I guess for some people, if sex isn't that important, it doesn't matter." I was digging myself a deeper hole with every word. "As long as you don't find each other repugnant." Gino lost it and laughed. I huffed out a breath, trying not to laugh too. Let's face it, that was a ridiculous conversation to have with your boss. "You are the greatest," I told him. "Let's go in and warm up."

Lou was in the audience. He didn't have a 'usual' table, but he was a noticeable guy. Gino made some comment welcoming (and thanking) our regulars, then introduced our first number. "Any movie fans out there? Yeah, me too. My husband and I like to watch movies at home mostly, but we went out to see 'The Martian.' Anybody see that? Good movie, right? So when we were putting together the set tonight I was thinking, what's a good song about solitude. Imagine being all alone like that, hoping someone was coming for you, but trying to be prepared if no one did. Let's start this off with Steve Perry's 'Foolish Heart.'"

There was some movement in the audience, maybe people who were surprised that we would go so far off the Sinatra track. Gino made it sound like this was a spur of the moment choice. But we'd had a couple of weeks to work on the arrangement, and I thought we turned out something that Mr. Sinatra would have been happy to sing. Anyway, it went over big, and after we finished, while we were waiting for the applause to fade, I looked at Lou. He was sitting forward with his elbows on the table, clasped hands in front of his

39

mouth, staring at me. When we made eye contact he blew me a kiss. When I got over that I glanced up and saw Gino smiling at me. I rolled my eyes to say 'I am toast.' He raised his eyebrows and nodded. Then he turned back to the mic, and we got down to the business of music.

I was unbelievably nervous after the show. We took our bows, the stage lights went off, we went back to the green room to freshen up. I was staring at myself in the mirror, thinking nothing useful, when Gino came up behind me and set his hands on my shoulders. "You look great," he said. "You always do. Where are you going for dinner?"

"Staying right here. Keeping it simple."

"What's the worst that can happen?"

I blinked. That was a question I had not asked myself. I thought it through. "I guess the worst is that we can't stand each other in bed and … then what?"

"Then you can decide if you want to keep being friends who meet up for a drink after a show from time to time, or not."

Put that way, it didn't sound so terrifying. If the worst outcome was the big, kind, smart, funny cop still wanted to hang out in the bar once in a while, that was a good outcome. And if he didn't want to, well, that said something too. "What are the odds."

Gino read my mind. "That you won't like each other in bed? I personally would not bet on that." He turned me around and hugged me. "Go get him, tiger." I laughed against his hair. He kissed my cheek and pushed me gently away.

God, I loved that man. I waved at Ruben and Oscar, who for some reason were still hanging around, squared my shoulders, and went out. Lou was waiting, at the mouth of the corridor that led to the green room. Looking terrific in a gray sport jacket over black jeans, with a sky-blue dress shirt and good shoes. "Every girl's crazy 'bout a sharp-dressed man," I quoted saucily as I went up to him.

"I'm only interested in one girl," he said, and offered his arm. I took it, trying to hide my swoon, and we walked out through the lounge. Being in a casino, of course, you basically have to cross the gaming floor to get from any one place to any other place. The restaurant we were going to was on the far side. "Great show tonight."

"How'd you like that opening number?"

"It was fantastic. I would never have thought of that for Gino. Did you do the arrangement?"

"He sang it for us, how he thought it should go. Then Oscar and I put something together. Ruben got pretty creative, I thought."

"The cymbal," Lou agreed. "He made it sing. And the snare. He's really good. You all are. That would make a great single."

"Huh! You think so?" I thought about it for a few seconds. I could definitely imagine hearing it on Siriusly Sinatra. A few of the tracks from 'What If It Were True' were showing up there, and one of the DJs had done a phone thing with Gino where they played the entire album, with chitchat between tracks. "I'll mention it to him. So what have you been up to since I saw you last."

That little bit of catching up got us to the restaurant. Then we had ordering to occupy us. We were in a booth, semicircular, one that four people could fit into. We might have sat across from each other, but we didn't. We sat side by side, at just that

41

little bit of an angle. I was close enough to feel his body heat. After a while, after wine arrived but before salad, he said, "I was really nervous about tonight."

"You?! Why?"

"Well, because I really like you, and we haven't done this before, and I feel like the stakes are kind of high."

I didn't want to admit it, but I figured I owed him the same kind of honesty. "I felt that too. I'm not sure why."

"Me either." He had one elbow on the table, his head propped on that hand, gazing at me with a faint smile. "The last time I took a girl to dinner I was not nervous."

"The last time a guy took me to dinner I was like, could we get this over with please." Lou laughed. I drank some wine. "Can I ask you something?"

"Of course."

"Why the police?"

"Hmm." He sat back, still angled toward me, his wrist still on the table. It occurred to me I had both elbows on the table, and the table was kind of a bridge between us in that moment, but the way I was leaning forward closed me off from him. Gino told us about body language, early on. He said, on stage you have to be open. The audience won't even realize why they're not connecting, but they won't. I didn't want that, so I took my inside elbow off the table and mirrored Lou's posture. His eyelids flickered and I could tell he understood. "I got hurt often enough and bad enough that I didn't want to stay with the Army for a full twenty. And, well." He glanced away for a second, then back. "I'm not a real political guy, but I couldn't help feeling that the places we were deployed were not

42

places we had any real business being. The police seemed like a good transitional profession."

"Seemed." It wasn't quite a question.

"I'm not sorry I joined the force. It's not my forever job. Not the way yours is."

"My God I love this job." Then our salads arrived, and I was hungry, so I dug into mine. Lou must have been hungry too. According to the catch-up report, he'd done some work on his house and then gone to the gym, all before reporting in. I hoped he didn't mind that the gym and I were barely-civil acquaintances. The server was paying attention, so our entrées arrived right after the salad plates were cleared. "I cannot imagine a job I would love more than working with Gino and the Rogues," I said after a while, when the inner woman was satisfied. Officer Gym Rat cleaned his plate before me, then sat quietly, giving me time. I appreciated not being hustled through the meal. "When I auditioned, Gino and I clicked right away. Ruben and Oscar are approximately the least chauvinistic musicians I've ever met. I mean, it's not only me, letting the girl take the lead in the trio. It's Gino. A lot of black and Latino guys would simply not be cool with backing up an out gay guy, even to get a sweet gig like this. And based on knowing them this long, they simply do not give a shit. It's *so nice* to not have any of that bullshit to deal with."

"Plus they all like your music."

"Yes! It's freaky!" He laughed. I drank the rest of my wine, shook my head to the raised eyebrows that seemed to ask if I wanted another glass. I was ready to go. I wasn't nervous anymore. "Where did you leave your ride?"

"It's at the station. I got a lift."

"Well. Is it time to see if you fit into my car?" *And then we can see if you fit into me.* Maybe he read my mind; he inhaled, his pupils dilated, and his lips parted. My God, he was sexy. It seemed like a long time before we were done with the whole paying-for-dinner thing and walking across the gaming floor again.

Needless to say, he fit into my car. About half an hour later, I stopped worrying about anything else. When I woke up the next morning and saw that big, tough, scarred, gorgeous cop in my bed, I said, "Jesus, I'm glad you're here."

IV – Lou

October 2015

I wish I could say that our first time was a slow, careful, mutual seduction. That we unwrapped each other like precious gifts, exploring and cherishing, and made love like angels. I can't say that. We fucked like animals.

Gloria opened the door to her apartment and gestured me in. I turned to watch her triple-lock the door. She turned to face me and said, "You're going to want to take your jacket off." She moved past me. "Everything else, too." She emptied her pockets onto the little kitchen table, then walked into the room I knew was the bedroom. I heard her shoes hit the floor while I was getting mine off. She went into the bathroom, but was out again before I had my pants off. I was trying to be organized. My hands were shaking. I went in there, scrubbed my teeth with a finger, had a piss, washed my hands, checked myself out. I still had my undershirt and briefs on, because … well, because. I didn't want to stroll into her bedroom naked, like I owned the place. Also I didn't know if she would leave the light on, and while she knew I had scars, knowing and seeing were two different things. I took a second to be grateful I'd shaved before going to the casino, then went to join her.

She was sitting cross-legged on the bed, completely naked. Her hair was down. A trio of pillar candles were lit, on the top of her dresser. I edged past the digital piano, not knowing what to say. She looked like a goddess. "What part of 'everything else' was unclear?"

I huffed out a laugh, nervousness abating, wondering if she could see my cock twitch at the thought of being naked with her. "You're in charge," I said, just to be clear.

"Okay. So get naked. What I'm seeing is great. Let's see the rest of it."

Oh lord. It is awkward getting boxer briefs off when you have a hard-on. She didn't laugh. She made a yummy sound and I had to remind myself to breathe. "You're so beautiful."

"You too. For the record, I won't get pregnant and I won't give you a disease. You can trust me."

I felt a little lightheaded now, because what I was hearing was 'we don't need a condom if you're clean.' I swallowed, inhaled, and said, "You can trust me too." I was still standing by the bed. I put one knee on it, dropping the lube by her leg. She glanced at it, then pushed up onto her knees and straight-up grabbed me, pulling me over, mouth going ravenously for mine. The next thing I knew I was on my back and she was on her knees over me, propped on one hand. Her other hand was between her legs, getting me in position. She brushed across me. "Jesus, Gloria." Wet, hot, starting to take me in. She put her other hand down and went for my mouth again, sinking onto me. Not too fast to enjoy it. Slowly, in fact. I thought *hell*, and was deeply grateful to the long-ago woman who'd told me nature needed a little help sometimes. I patted around for the lube.

Gloria didn't notice. She hissed a little. "Fuck, you're fucking huge."

I held her off with one hand. "Hang on baby." Got the lube and squeezed some into my hand. Slicked myself up. Then slid my fingers through her, and oh holy night, the heat of her just about did me in. "Try now."

She was staring into my eyes. "Ungh. God *damn,* Lou." Still slow, but now her eyes were half closed and her mouth was half open. "Yes. Oh my God yes."

I didn't know how she was even making words. Her knees were clamped to the outside of my thighs and she was rocking. Grinding against me, every breath vocal, the pitch ratcheting up. I had one hand in her hair, gripping it to keep it out of our mouths. The other hand was somewhere, I don't remember. Maybe holding onto the bed somehow because this felt like rafting over a waterfall. I was losing it. "Oh God."

"Yes yes now, fucking now, yes –"

"God!"

"Jesus!"

And there we went. I don't know how fast, exactly, but it couldn't have been even five minutes. She didn't collapse on me. She reared up, this primeval amazement in the candlelight, and arched her back. My cock, which should have been lying down for a nap, twitched again. "Gloria."

"What happens if I stay right here?" She sounded breathless, but more rational than I felt. She contracted around me. Between us, things were so wet down there that I could hear it. I didn't think I was good for a repeat quite this fast. And the next time, I wanted to control it. Wanted to try, at least. I put my hands on her hips, let them wander. Up and down her thighs. Down in front, around in back. What a magnificent double handful of ass. I bracketed her waist with my hands, thumbs rubbing lightly over the swell of her belly, then knuckles across the bottom of her ribcage. Finally reaching her breasts. Those were amazing too. I was almost surprised she didn't have any other tattoos. Usually a person with ink on their neck did not start there. Of course, I hadn't yet seen her bare back. I traced one of those thorny stems, one that draped from her collarbone around her shoulder. She still had me inside, and I could tell I was at least half hard. Still, or again. She was watching my hands. "How long has it been for you?"

I looked up into those big dark eyes. "A little less than a year."

She rotated her hips. "This guy thinks that was too long."

"He's had things to say ever since I kissed you." She grinned. "Do you have any other ink?"

"You'll see." Then she reached behind her, spreading some of that wetness over my balls. I don't think I had ever made that exact sound before. She was going lower. I opened my legs a little, bent my knees, got my heels against the bed and pushed up. God, all that juice, and her fingers *there*. A woman hadn't touched me there in a very long time. I'd forgotten what it felt like. "God almighty, Lou, if you could see your face."

"If you could see yours," I managed. She leaned down to kiss me, which was very nice except it meant she took her hand away. And then she disengaged, and I made another really undignified sound. But she wasn't stopping. Oh lord, no, she was moving south, using her mouth on my chest, kissing that scar under my ribs. Kissing and licking my cock, then taking it in her mouth with another yummy sound. Letting me go again – I was panting, almost whimpering – pushing my thigh up to get to everything. "Holy Jesus Christ."

She stopped long enough to say, "I thought you were Jewish."

"Dad is. Don't stop."

"I'll get you off this way someday." Back to my balls, a return to my cock. I was so painfully hard I couldn't believe it. Teeth and tongue on my nipples, one after the other, and I was flailing. Then her mouth on mine and a hand under my shoulder. She was on her back and I was between her legs, going in fast and hard. "Holy fuck! Lou!"

My cock felt a foot long and I was pounding into her, completely out of control again. She had one leg hooked over my thigh, the other heel digging into the bed, her hands braced against the wall to keep her head from slamming into it. We were both making the porniest porn sounds you ever heard. I was not getting enough air. I was not capable of trying to make this good for her. I was a machine with only one purpose: to come as hard as possible. When I started to go and my rhythm broke, her back arched. I can't even describe that beautiful line of throat, bosom, ribs. I yelled something, my own body arching away. Sunk so deep in her that my pubic bone was right against her clit, and I was pouring into her, and she gasped out a "Yes."

A minute or so later, she gave me a shove. I crawled off her, still incapable of speech. My whole body ached. "My poor neighbors." Her tone did not convey genuine regret. I produced a soundless laugh. She patted me randomly. "Thank God the bedrooms don't back up to each other."

"They don't?"

"Nope. Some kind soul laid out these one-bedrooms so that you can hear your neighbors fucking if they do it while you're having dinner." I was laughing for real now. "I haven't made that much noise for a really long time."

"The last time, you were in the kitchen." She smacked me, not too hard. I rolled onto my back, somewhat carefully. "That was unbelievable."

"Mmm. It was all right."

I laughed again. "Think we could try it again sometime? See if I can do better?"

"Jesus, Lou, if you did any better I'd be broken in half and turned inside out. Thanks for the lube, that was timely." She stretched, wriggling her back, then relaxed again. "I should pull up the covers." She didn't move. I sat up, again carefully, and started to fix the sheet and quilt situation. I felt Gloria's hand on my back. "What the fuck, Lou."

"Afghanistan."

"What even makes a scar like that?"

"Traumatically losing a kidney. We had a good field hospital, considering." I was still sitting up, still looking away.

"Jesus H. Christ." After a few seconds: "Which came first?"

"Iraq first. That was shrapnel from an IED. Two soldiers in my squad died and another guy lost a leg."

"This." Fingers still on the scar. "Was this the end, or did you go back after?"

"This was the end. I could have gone back. I thought that actually losing a body part was a good sign it was time to quit."

An irritated noise. "I do not think 'quit' is the correct word, Lou." She stroked her hand all over my back, finding the edges of bones, tracing the outlines of muscles. "Your body is beautiful."

I turned around. Her hand stayed on me, but in a comforting way, not a suggestive way. I don't know how I could tell the difference. "Yours is beautiful too." We gazed at each other for a few seconds. "Okay if I stay?"

"For fuck's sake, Lou, of course it is. Could you blow out the candles?"

So I got out of bed, made a comment about needing to stretch, blew out the candles. Bent (slowly, carefully; my spine wasn't damaged but some muscles and nerves were) to touch my toes, did a hip-flexor stretch with one knee and then the other on the bed. She made some crack about already being as stretched out as she wanted to get. I got back into bed, my skin now cool, and pressed up against her. She yelped. Then she wrapped her arm over the one I had around her waist, making a sound I could only describe as 'contented.' How did I know what a contented Gloria sounded like? Could I ever, ever have imagined this moment? "My mother's going to love you," I murmured against her hair. I think she was already asleep. A moment later, I was too.

IV – Gloria

October 2015

Let me simply say that our porntastic thirty-six-hour First Real Date effectively banished any worries I had about whether we would get along in bed as well as we got along out of it. The next couple of weeks did nothing to change my mind about that. If we had not both been in possession of full-time jobs, one of which had a schedule that was all-of-a-suddenly annoyingly irregular, we probably would have fucked ourselves into an early grave. All I needed was to hear his voice on the phone and I was wet. We had sex in every position, and in some very inappropriate locations. By which I mean, for example, in the green room (not during a show). In my car (which was uncomfortable and hilarious, and yet we both got off). In the alley behind La Cholla, and it was pure luck that we didn't get cited for indecency, because Lou still had his hand under my skirt and hadn't done up his jeans when the patrol car cruised by.

He said "Shit" and got his arm around my neck like we were only kissing, turned his head and did that chin-lift thing, like oh hey how ya doing. The cop in the car must have recognized him; I heard a bark of laughter, and he drove on.

"You're going to hear about that later," I said, trying not to absolutely guffaw.

"Thank you for wearing this dress." I pulled a bandanna out of my pocket and handed it to him. He wiped his hand, then me, then put my underwear back the way he'd found it and tidied himself up for a second while I made sure he was in shadow. Then he zipped up again, folded the bandanna, and stuck it in his back pocket. "Thanks for that, too. And thank you for being tall, so I can fuck you standing up in an alley."

Pure romance, if you could see his face when he said that, which I could. And hear the caressing tone of his voice. God, I was crazy about him. "Um, you're welcome. Did we already have dinner, or did we do this first." I knew, of course. He'd leaned over to kiss me when I got out of my car, and since that parking lot was brightly lit a brief excursion to the alley had seemed prudent.

"If you can't remember, I must be doing something right." He was smiling.

"You're doing everything right. Come on, I'm hungry." We moseyed around to the front, went into the deliciously-fragrant restaurant, said Hi to Salma, and went to the table that Lou said was his usual. "Is Gonzo coming?"

"As far as I know. You look great."

I don't know how he could read my mind like that. "You look like we've been fucking in an alley." I took one of the paper napkins off the table and wiped away some stray lipstick on his face. And neck. The shirt was on its own. He was snickering, which gave me a very bad feeling. I said "Be right back" and made tracks for the bathroom. Said "Holy shit" and spent a few minutes trying to make myself look less like I'd been fucking in an alley. It was impossible to be mad about it. I was going to have to start carrying a mirror. Once I was less embarrassingly obvious, I went out to our table, where I found a bowl of fresh guacamole, a basket of chips, a bottle of Corona, and a somewhat-penitent Lou. He started to apologize and I waved it off. "I have the power to say no," I reminded him. "If I recall correctly, it was my idea to go back there."

"Still. I shouldn't act like a teenager."

I loaded a chip with guac, crunched it down, and had a swallow of beer. "Did you do shit like that in high school?"

"Afraid so." He couldn't hide the smile. I bet he was a dreamboat when he was a teenager.

"I want to see a picture of you twenty years ago."

"Okay. I'll get you one."

That was unexpectedly easy. "Want to see one of teenage me?"

"Of course I do." He ate some chips and guac while I dug out my phone and found a picture of the high-school jazz ensemble. Handed it over and waited. "Wow, Gloria, look at you. What a beauty. Did you rule that group too?"

I swooned a little. I always did when he called me beautiful. "I did rule it, that year. Then the next year we got this transfer student who played trumpet, and a bunch of other things. The fucker was really fucking good, and he knew it. He was hot-looking, too. So he kind of ruled senior year."

"Was he a jerk?"

"Oh, no. Actually I could imagine Gino being a lot like this guy at that age. Except this guy wasn't gay. At least I don't think so. He and I never had a thing but he always had a gang of girls, and not in the gal-pal way." I ate a couple more chips, trying to get my share before Officer Loves Guac got it all. "Actually now that I think about it, I wonder. I never vibed him because he wasn't my type. Wow, maybe he was!"

"Was it the kind of school where being out would have been a problem?"

"It sure was. I wonder where he is now. I may have to internet stalk him."

Lou was laughing. "I do that sometimes. Look up people who were interesting back in the day."

"Ever find out anything you wish you hadn't?" I scooped up the last bit of guac. "I found out one of my favorite teachers lost their son. He was away at college and got killed in a traffic accident. I'd never met him and I hadn't seen my teacher for years. I didn't know what to do, so I didn't do anything. I found out long after the fact. It seemed like it would be cruel to bring it up just so I could say I was sorry, you know?"

He nodded, drank some beer, and didn't say anything for a minute. "I found out one of my friends from the high-school football team committed suicide."

"Oh, shit, Lou."

"It was while I was overseas. He'd been drafted, played professional ball for a couple of years. Then he was injured, really bad, all the ligaments in his knee were blown. I didn't even know until I saw the story about him and the gun. That was three years after it happened. Before Afghanistan." He drank the rest of his beer. "Like you say. It was so long after the fact that it felt like saying anything to his parents would be for me, not for them. It had been years since the last time I looked him up."

Salma came to get our order. No doubt she could tell we were talking about serious shit. She told us Gonzo wouldn't make it, he was way out of town. Lou nodded and thanked her. A minute later a couple fresh beers were on the table. I said, "How close were you to that guy? In high school, I mean."

"Not that close. That's what I regretted most. It's like, if we'd been better friends, if we'd been closer, if we'd stayed in touch, maybe I could have been the voice telling him there was something to live for." He shrugged. "They said he would never have played again, but the rest of his body still worked. I can't imagine doing that."

"Me neither. But then, I could still do ninety percent of what I love if I were a paraplegic." I shook myself a little. "Did you have close friends in the Army?"

Lou relaxed. "Oh sure. It was kind of like showbiz, though, from what I've heard. You get sent out on a mission, or even just to a new base, and you're with a new group of people. You have to be best friends, absolutely loyal, right away. You have to work together and help each other and protect each other, even if you stand back and think, I would hate this fucker if I met him on the street." I snorted a laugh into my beer. Lou smiled. "You should try to find that trumpet guy. Who knows, maybe he wants to come to Vegas and play on Gino Corsetti and The Desert Rogues' next record."

"Who knows. Maybe he does!" It was kind of a fun thought. And if Lou really didn't mind, maybe kind of a fun second chance. "I never got to know him that well, obviously, if I'm not even sure what gender he was. Is. If I find him I'll tell him I have a boyfriend." Lou laughed. "I mean, for all we know he's been carrying a torch for me all these years. It would be a big old mess to say hey come to Vegas and play with us and then find out, whoops, he's camping outside my apartment." Food was delivered, not a moment too soon, because obviously I was getting silly. That sad look across the table was gone, though. To keep it gone I invented this speech about my boyfriend the cop, and then I started riffing on how that could be the next concept album. That led to 'I am the very model of a modern traffic officer.' Lou finally told me to stop after almost inhaling some mole sauce.

When we finally left the restaurant he walked me out, carrying the leftovers, which he then put in my car because the odds were very good that he'd be at my place to eat them within a day and half. Then he hugged me for quite a while. "I know what you were up to," he said against my hair. "And I appreciate it."

"You can't save the world, Officer Big Heart. It's awfully nice that you want to."

"Eh. Whatever. I've been a lucky man. Sometimes it seems like I've had more than my share of luck."

"You work your ass off," I pointed out. "And you almost got killed twice that I know of, and probably more times that you haven't told me about. I vote for hoarding the rest of your luck for yourself. And me. And okay, maybe Gonzo."

"Stop," he said, laughing again. He kissed me. "You're on a roll tonight."

"Two Coronas on an almost-empty stomach after my big handsome cop boyfriend gave me an orgasm in the alley. You'd better follow me home so you can arrest me if I swerve into oncoming traffic."

He kissed me again. "I will follow you home, but I'm not coming up. I'm on at oh eight hundred tomorrow."

"Fuck that fucking fucker!" I didn't even know who was making the schedule lately. I only knew I hated him. Or her. I did not hate Lou, though, so I kissed him one more time and then got in the car. "Get as much sleep as you can, Officer Kravitz." I did not mention that it would make more sense for him to stay overnight with me than to head back home. I might think I was ready to cohabit, but maybe he wasn't, and we hadn't even talked about it, and everything was so new that I needed to chill. Before I closed the door I looked up at him, thought frighteningly forever thoughts, and said, "Be careful out there."

"Always. Good night, Gloria Louise."

"Good night, Officer." Door closed, strapped in, key turned, engine running, in gear. Backing away from the second-best thing that had ever happened to me. So very glad that it was only for a day or two.

The next day, Gino couldn't believe I said that. "Second-best? You're crazy about him!"

We were out in the parking lot, as per usual pre-show. I hadn't given him the previous evening's adventures in full detail, only a summary. Not even to Gino would I confess some of the literally law-breaking shenanigans I'd been up to with my cop.

He'd agreed that I should look up the trumpet player, and now he was about ready to spank me. I almost cracked up. "Well, Gino, you're the *first* best thing that ever happened to me." Of course he melted. And he hadn't put his Sinatra-blue contact lenses in yet, so I got the full benefit of his soft brown Bambi eyes. I leaned a little closer, bumped his shoulder with mine. "I am, possibly, the luckiest girl in the world." He made a sound of assent, which made me laugh. We went back inside to get ready to play.

V – Lou

November 2015

The switch to second watch took some adjustment, mostly on my part. Okay, entirely on my part, and mostly because the past month had been so erratic that I didn't even know when I was supposed to be trying to sleep. Gloria didn't change a thing about her routine, and that made it easier. The bigger adjustment was the mental shift that came when she handed me a key to her apartment.

We were in bed at the time, and I was half-asleep because she'd just fucked my brains out. When I felt something small, hard, and cold land on my chest I made some kind of sound and she laughed. "Leave it there for a second, it'll get warm."

I put a hand on the thing, picked it up, and squinted at it. There wasn't a lot of light, but it looked familiar. I turned my head and saw her watching me. "Are you sure about this?"

"You mean, considering past mistakes in the field of key-sharing?" I thought for a second she was going to say something snarky, but she didn't. She said, "I should never have given a key to anybody but you."

I dropped the key on the nightstand on my side – maybe I could call it my nightstand, now – and rolled over to wrap her in my arms. I wanted to say 'I love you' so bad I could taste it. "Could I take you somewhere the next time we both have the same day off?"

"Sure." She let me kiss her for a minute. "Where?"

"I want to show you my house."

"Oh!" She knew about the house, of course. We'd talked about it a lot. Obviously, she also knew about the

59

motorcycle. "By take me somewhere I hope you mean I'm driving."

I laughed against her mouth. "Maybe it's time for me to get a car."

"Not on my account. Go to sleep."

"Mmm." My glorious Glory. I hoped she would like the house. I went to sleep remembering the last time we had dinner at La Cholla, with Salma hanging over the counter laughing while Gloria and Gonzo got silly in Spanglish.

Once the date was locked down (which I could do with some confidence; it was rare for me to get assigned to a schedule-breaking investigative team) I was a bundle of nerves. I told my mother Gloria was getting the tour soon. Mom, of course, wanted to see what I'd done since the last round of pictures. I said no. She yelled at me. I said, "Mom, I swear, nothing's changed. Not a thing. I haven't painted, I haven't bought more furniture, it's all the same."

"What the hell are you waiting for?" Then, before I could answer, "Are you going to let her pick the colors and shit?"

I knew that saying yes to that was the same as saying I was going to propose. "Yes."

"Louis Emmanuel. Does she know you love her?"

"I'm going to tell her if she likes the house."

"Why wouldn't she like the house? It's a great house!"

"Mom," I said affectionately, "it's a ways out of town and it's isolated. She might hate the location even if she loves the house."

"What're you going to do if that happens? Sell the house?"

I really didn't want to do that. "I don't know." Then I changed the subject, kind of. "She gave me a key to her apartment."

"What does that mean."

"Well, I think it means I can go in whenever I want."

Mom made an irritated noise. "Aside from that, smarty pants."

"I'm hoping it means the same thing me not painting the house means." I listened to her laugh. "I love you, Mom. Tell Dad I said hi. I'll let you know how it goes."

"Don't screw this up." She disconnected. I made a rude comment to the empty air and put my phone away. I really hoped Gloria didn't hate the house, or the location. At least I knew she liked Gonzo, and he was crazy about her. Salma liked her, too. If things worked out for us I had another idea, which might be a little out there, but it tracked with what I'd begun thinking of as the Next Thing. The next thing I wanted to try doing with my life.

When I decided on joining the police, I didn't expect to make a twenty-year career of it. It was like I told Gloria, a way to make a transition from military to civilian life. Still serving, still contributing, but a step back. I'd thought I might put in a dozen years. After the first two, I'd thought maybe six. And now I thought four would be plenty. I was positive I didn't want to try for promotion. It was satisfying work but not as satisfying as rebuilding the house had been. So now I was thinking I'd go for a contractor's license. Maybe put myself through home-building boot camp with Gonzo and a couple of his buddies, an electrician and a plumber. We could put another house on my land. If Gonzo and Salma wanted to live there, great. If not, maybe one of Gloria's Rogues would like it. I knew Oscar's wife because she was on the force. I'd only met Ruben's girlfriend Carla in passing, but I got the idea the two of them were in the same place as Gonzo and Salma: building up a stake to settle down together.

Hell, maybe we could build our own little village out there. Twelve acres was plenty of space for four houses, if everyone was friendly. I went to get ready for work, laughing at myself for daydreaming. There were worse ways to spend my time. Before I left, I took a minute to study the house, trying to see it through fresh eyes. The patchwork stucco made it look shabby and unfinished, but the bones were good. I hoped Gloria would like the yard. It was so not the usual desert yard. When I got the place, there was a hedge of gnarly mesquite all the way around the one-acre lot. We trimmed that up after the heavy machinery work was done. All the scrap wood was in a shed, waiting for the day I got myself a smoker.

To fill in the front yard I'd consulted a native-plants website. The desert willows I'd planted, three of them, were now a dozen feet tall. They sat in a meadow of sages and grasses. Low maintenance, drought-tolerant, and amazingly pretty in the spring when the trees were blooming. I had a power supply and water connection ready to put in a water feature someday. It was a lot like Sergei's backyard, actually. I was hoping that would be a selling point for Gloria.

Finally the day came. A Monday, Gloria's usual day off. She drove, I navigated, we didn't talk much. I was hoping she couldn't tell how nervous I was. Out of the blue, she said, "I'm nervous."

"What? Why?"

"I have this really whack idea of a desert house. I've lived in the city for fifteen years."

For some reason that made me smile. "You can see the city at night. Here's the turn." Off the main road, onto the one that went to my property and then past it for a mile or so before turning to gravel. It was traversable in a four-wheel-drive, but I hadn't yet seen anyone coming from the other direction. My acres weren't fenced. I had 'private property' signs up at the corners. As far as I knew, the only trespassers were coyotes, the four-legged kind. I walked the whole perimeter fairly often, but there was a good bit of the twelve acres that I'd only seen from the air, when I had a chance to go up for medevac EMT training.

"Is this it?" The words alone could be taken all kinds of ways. Gloria's tone, however, was very encouraging. "What a great yard! It's like Sergei's!" She pulled into the driveway and turned off the car.

"When we went over there that time I thought, oh hey, those are my trees." I was smiling with pleasure and relief, because she was getting out of the car and heading for the yard. It was easy in street shoes, with a sort of suggestion of a path, surfaced with decomposed granite, winding through the knee-high plants. I could see when she spotted the area I'd mentally designated for the water feature. "That's the window from the kitchen. I thought it would be nice to sit in there with coffee and watch the critters once I get a little fake creek going."

"That would be great. My grandma in Santa Fe has something like that. She only has a tiny lot, though. This feels like the whole world."

"It's pretty big," I agreed. "I didn't want to live somewhere with other houses right on top of me." I turned toward the front door. "Want to see inside?"

"Definitely. What color are you going to paint it?"

"What would you suggest?" I said that while I was unlocking the door, not looking at her. I felt her sharp glance, though. "I haven't painted inside, either."

"Well, I know you've been – holy shit, Lou." She stopped three steps in, looking across the main living area to the wall of glass and the courtyard beyond. "This is like something out of Architectural Digest."

I was absurdly pleased. I mean, she'd said some nice things to me by now, but this was something I made. Nobody but my family and Gonzo had really seen it. "Come see the rest." I gave her the tour. She said almost nothing. The tail of the F was the garage, utility rooms, and powder room. The master suite was the bottom stroke of the F. Then the living-dining-kitchen space, anchored by a big double-sided rock fireplace. The top stroke of the F was the guest suite, a.k.a. Gonzo's room, and the third bedroom. Or – as I hoped – the music room.

"Jesus Christ," she said, after a few minutes. She kept circling, looking out one window after another. "Who gets this room?"

The look of naked covetousness on her face made the decision for me. "I was hoping that would be you. It's soundproofed. We could get a piano. I love you." She threw herself at me. I staggered back against the closet wall, laughing.

"I love you too," she said after a while. We were still upright, barely. "Can I live with you?"

"Roger that." I kissed her again, for a few more minutes. "Jesus. I should have put a couch in here. Something." She was laughing under her breath. "I didn't buy anything because I was hoping you'd want to choose your own."

"What will you do if everything's red and black?"

"I don't give a fuck if the place looks like a deck of cards, as long as you're happy."

She laughed again. "God, you're so great. I won't do that. Let's go back to your room." I thought that was a terrific idea. It took us a while to get there, because on our way through she suggested painting the living room hot pink, and we had to fake-argue about that. Then she said midnight blue for our bedroom, because she was always going to be a night owl. We didn't argue about that. We stopped talking altogether.

It was midafternoon before we wandered back out to the kitchen. I made some coffee, and pulled some food out of the fridge. We sat and ate in front of the window, discussing the pros and cons of man-made waterfalls. I told her about the smoker I wanted to get. She interrogated me on my grilling skills. I told her about maybe building another house or three. I was one hundred percent in love.

V – Gloria

December 2015

I hadn't moved in with Lou yet the day the Grammy nominations were announced. Not because I didn't want to, but between getting his house painted inside and out, and giving notice to my landlord, and a few other things, it was going to be Christmas week. Anyway, he was back on third watch, and he came through the door quietly, as usual – because I was usually asleep at this hour – and then stopped short. "Gloria? Is everything okay?"

I raised my coffee mug in a sort of casual salute and said, "Want to go to L.A. with me in February?"

He closed the door, clearly reassured but also clearly puzzled. "What's in L.A. in February?"

"The Grammy Awards."

Instant comprehension. God, I loved a smart man. "No fucking way. The record?"

"The record." I was grinning behind my mug. Then I set it down, because he was on the move, and a second later he had me out of my chair and in a bear hug. I squealed as quietly as possible, giggled through about a dozen kisses, and gasped for breath when he finally let me plop back down. "I called Gino the second I saw it. He was like, eh? What? I'm going over there, the guys are going. I know you need to sleep but I couldn't wait to tell you."

"That is unbelievably great. I mean, it's not unbelievable because it's a terrific record. But wow! That's awesome!" He locked his service weapon in the new little safe as he spoke. That bit of multitasking didn't bother me at all. (The gun actually didn't bother

66

me. It was his idea to get the safe.) He said, "I'm so proud of you."

"Thank you. Yes. Yes, it is awesome. I wrote the title track of a Grammy-nominated record, and if I don't get that side hustle writing for 'Behind the Strip' I will demand an explanation." I felt a little bit high. It was the three of us Rogues up for that gig, incidental music for a streaming series that was going to be filmed in the city. It was based on that series of newspaper articles by Kathy Donovan, or on her book, or both. Anyway it was a thing. She'd finagled herself a job as the head writer, with a producer credit on top of that. She was going to be so thrilled for Gino. I dragged my mind back to the gorgeous man leaning against the kitchen counter. Broad chest, long legs, and warm eyes. He didn't look all that tired. "Are you tired?" A slow smile. "Are you hungry?" A slow shake of the head. That was probably a lie, but he could probably tell where I was going with this, and he was never that hungry. "Want to help me celebrate?" He started taking off his uniform, right there in the kitchen.

About an hour later I got out of the apartment. Lou was still awake, having breakfast (or dinner, depending on how you look at it) and I needed to get across town to Gino and Sergei's. I stopped on the way for orange juice and cheap sparkling wine for mimosas. I might have screamed to myself in the car. I'd sent texts to my family, warning them I'd be offline most of the day and suggesting we talk tomorrow. By then I'd've had a full night's sleep, and a day to get used to this amazeballs Thing.

It got even more amazeballs later, when we dragged ourselves to work. The casino's entertainment director was in our green room waiting for us. They were going to send us all to Los Angeles. Travel, hotel, the works. They were revising the marketing for our show immediately. They were planning to book a fill-in artist to cover that weekend, but also to cover a couple of days a month going forward so we could work on the new album. I didn't know they even knew there *was* a new one in the works.

Gino had been none too pleased to get my call at five-thirty-ish in the morning, but boy was he in a good mood that night. He only mentioned the nomination once per show, which I thought was unnecessarily modest, and as always he threw a lot of kind words our way. He sang as well as he ever did, which was better than ninety-nine percent of the singers on Earth, and he looked like a million bucks even a few hours shy of enough sleep. When we wrapped it up for the night, we were all feeling the long day and I at least already had a mimosa hangover, but we were some happy campers. There were so many things I wanted to say to those guys. I settled for some heartfelt thank-yous, complete with hugs. Then we strolled out to the parking lot and said 'see you Tuesday,' and anyone would have thought it was a normal day.

My parents were unusually criticism-free when I spoke to them (separately; they're divorced). My grandma in Santa Fe was her usual Team Gloria self. All of them knew about Lou and the imminent cohabitation. Grandma Ynez was one hundred percent in favor. She'd been suggesting it ever since I sent a picture (to which her reply text was: *ay papi*. I laughed for days).

Lou had asked if I wanted to go anywhere for Christmas, and I kind of didn't because my parents (both in Phoenix) did not make that shit easy, and Santa Fe was too far to drive. But then he said, well, I know this guy with his own plane and he's working on getting a commercial license. So the long story short on that was, we were flying to Santa Fe. Grandma was so excited. I was too, honestly, though slightly nervous about a private flight. I'd never been on a plane that small, and had only flown a few times in my life anyway. Fortunately I had the whole moving-in thing to distract me.

I didn't have much furniture, and what I did have wasn't worth moving. I told my neighbors, and easily found people willing to (in a couple of cases, eager to) take everything off my hands. That left me with kitchen stuff, bathroom stuff, clothes, a fuck-ton of music, my digital piano and its stand, my computer, and the small gun safe. Oh yes, and a carton of assorted liquor. It would all fit into a baby U-Haul, with room to spare. Once we had a for-sure move-in date, we couldn't avoid the Furniture Talk anymore. "I don't want to buy a bunch of cheap crap again," I said. "Your house is too nice. Most of my shit's going to go in the music room. Where in the hell can we find decent stuff? I need a computer desk and shelving, more than anything. I'd like a little table where I could sit with the guys. Three good task chairs. I have money for it," I added, because I didn't want him to think I'd ask him to pay for my work space. "The only reason I didn't get better stuff before is it wouldn't have fit the space and I always intended to move."

Lou patiently waited while I got all that out, and did not point out that my 'only reason' was actually two reasons. "I've been thinking about the problem," he said. "Gonzo has a proposal for you."

I pretended to be shocked. "Does Salma know?"

That got me a smile from the big guy. "Come over here." Since 'over here' was on the bed I kind of wondered if Gonzo's proposal required some kind of demonstration. But after I was comfortably cuddled up beside Lou, he lifted a graph notebook (which he always had with him, so I'd stopped noticing it) off the nightstand and flipped through a few pages. When he got to the page he wanted, he handed it to me. "This is a floor plan and the next couple pages are elevations."

By now I knew what that meant. I studied the floor plan. It looked a bit crowded with a full-size upright piano in the room. I flipped to the next pages and said "Oh!" A bunch of curved arrows showed how the digital piano was on a shelf that would roll back under the work surface. So was the computer keyboard. A table would fold up to the wall. Two of the task chairs could be stowed in the closet. A deep cabinet, deep enough for music scores or LPs – I didn't even have a player, and I only had a few records, but I treasured them – was placed under the two windows on the courtyard wall, making a window seat. Everything was accessible, the doorway was unimpeded, and all the surfaces had rounded corners. It was obvious this would have to be completely custom. It was also obvious that someone had taken about a million measurements in order to produce to-scale drawings. I didn't need to ask who that someone was. "How long would this take?"

"It could be completely done by the time we go to L.A. Could you set up in the living room till then?"

That was longer than I wanted, but faster than I'd feared. I could continue working with the guys at Gino's house. We wanted to start recording the new album in January, so we couldn't – or rather, I didn't want to – wait till this was done. Sergei wouldn't mind, especially if we were mostly there when he wasn't. I realized I hadn't answered Lou, and that he was looking at me with a hint of anxiety. "Yes. I could use the living room for a while. We're about to get serious on the new record, but we can mostly rehearse at Gino's. Ruben and Oscar are already working out their parts. This is great, by the way." Lou relaxed, almost imperceptibly. I wondered if he was afraid he'd overstepped. "For the record, actually starting this work before I knew what was going on would have pissed me off even if I liked the result. However, doing it this way is perfect. Thank you." I leaned over to kiss him. "I haven't had somebody else thinking of what might be good for me since I lived with Grandma. It's a trip." He laughed, took the notebook out of my hand and dropped it on the nightstand, then kissed me again.

I told the guys about that the next time I saw them. Ruben and Oscar were already envious of Gino's music room, and now they were having a fit. They bitched about how far out of town mine was going to be, to cover that up. I did not mention to them the half-formed idea Lou had shared with me, of building a little village out there. Neither of us knew if these guys would like the idea at all. They both rented, here in the city, and I would be the first to admit that when we were all together we talked mostly about music. It was never about, you know, do you ever think of buying a house. Lou had some kind of reason for not wanting to bring it up yet. I thought he wanted to hit that four-year mark with the LVPD. Plus, we hadn't even lived together for more than a minute. Once I was in and we found our groove, I was sure he'd talk to Gonzo first. About a house, I mean. The talk about my music room was going to happen immediately. Might have already happened.

God, I couldn't wait to be actually living with him. I'd lived with someone before, for almost four years. It wasn't a terrible experience by any means. It was straight out of college, and I'd known almost immediately that this was not forever, but we were good roommates who had good sex, and when he fell in love with someone else we parted friends. All that time I was hustling. When I occasionally looked around and thought 'should I not be trying to find The One' I always looked back down at my work and decided that was more important. It never seemed possible to have both. It never occurred to me that maybe The One would be The One because he understood my work, and what it meant to me, and what I needed in order to do it.

The guys since then were all – okay, mostly – decent guys. But each of them had wanted something I didn't have, or couldn't give, and finally someone wanted the me that was. It was spectacular.

There were moments when I thought 'you have only known him for a few months' and wondered if I was out of my mind. But the thing was, it didn't feel rushed. We did a lot of talking before we went to bed, and we did a fair amount of dating before we said I Love You. If that particular thing coincided with the invitation to cohabit it was probably only because, on the one hand, Lou could see from my reaction that I loved his house, and that was important. On the other hand, I could see that he wanted me – including a piano and all that noise – in his house, and that was important.

Pile that on top of good manners, good friendship skills, a good work ethic, and great sex and you had a mountain of reasons to be in love.

VI – Lou

December 2015

Gloria did track down the trumpet guy, who turned out to be living in Los Angeles. He said he was glad she got in touch, and indicated that he would not at all mind working on a new all-original concept album with Gino and the gang. She gave me his data, all she had anyway, knowing I would run him. I didn't really expect to find a problem. Anybody with that much stuff on the internet couldn't be too concerned with keeping secrets. Facebook, Twitter, Instagram, YouTube, and a fan club site, all chock-full of comments and pictures, plus the occasional post from the man himself.

He'd been a professional musician for eighteen years. His website was not an artistic triumph, but it thoroughly accounted for those years. Artists he'd worked with, recordings he'd played on, tours, concerts, film and TV gigs. His name was Scott Easton, and it still wasn't clear what gender he was. I have to say he put the 'sex' in 'metrosexual.' I am straight as a two-by-twelve but this guy was smoking hot. The image on his home page was a full-length photo of him in a well-cut ivory suit, leaning his shoulder against a wall with one hand in his trouser pocket and the other holding his trumpet down by his leg. He wasn't looking at the camera. Instead he was looking off to the side, with a faint smile on his face, as if he'd been talking to someone out of frame. He had long hair, twisted back in a man bun that should have been annoying and wasn't. Blond on top, darker behind his ears, dark eyes. He wore glasses. Had a couple days' growth of facial hair. No tie, shirt unbuttoned at the neck. It all should have added up to pain-in-the-ass hipster posing, but it looked totally natural. Maybe because the wall he was leaning against was in what looked like some shitty dressing room. The image was cropped but you could see a few inches of a big mirror with other people reflected in it. I had to look at that and think, this is the actual guy, doing what he does, loving it. A real musician. It was, in other words, no surprise at all that Gloria remembered him.

I told her that the background check showed no reason to worry about booking him for the record, and minded my own business from that point. I had too much going on to be wondering about a random trumpet player, even if he did look like that. I had an opportunity to renew my EMT certification, I was keeping an eye on painters, I was getting Gonzo rolling on the music room, and I was arguing with my parents about why I wasn't bringing Gloria to New Jersey for Christmas.

I also took a page from Gloria's book and tracked somebody down. This was someone I hadn't entirely lost touch with. Facebook was, for me, a way to occasionally catch up with the high (and sometimes low) points in the lives of old friends, family members, and people I'd gotten to know over the years who weren't 'friends' in the real-world sense. Generally that was because we simply didn't live close enough together. But I felt it was better to be internet friends with somebody than not to be friends at all, because for one thing you never knew if you were going to be in Maine or Seattle or France or San Diego, and it would be nice to know someone there when you were.

Anyway, this was the guy I'd told her about who lost his leg in Iraq. He was in San Diego, and the last time we'd actually spoken was two years ago, but we'd been in touch online. I sent him a PM asking when would be a good time to call and he got back to me with a few options. So the next time I was not at work while Gloria was, I called him. He picked right up. "Captain Kravitz! What's new?"

"Lieutenant Sorenson, I'm in love."

"There's a lot of that going around."

"What, you too?"

"No, this buddy of mine, we met in rehab. He was Special Forces, Afghanistan. You might know him. Javier Bernal. He lost his below the knee, lucky fucker."

"I don't think I know him. I'll look him up though. You're doing good?"

"Oh yeah, doing good. Bernal's fiancée is this hot blonde massage therapist and she keeps finding me dates. The last one is an accident investigator for the NTSB, smart as a whip and has a pilot's license." He went on about this woman for a while, which made me doubt his story about not being in love. "Her name is Mai Tsao and I'm going to see her again soon."

"Well, good for you. Maybe she can fly you over to Vegas sometime."

"Yeah, maybe. So tell me about yours." I tried to keep it brief, literally watching the clock on my computer screen so I wouldn't go over three minutes because if I didn't check myself I could talk about Gloria for hours. Then I asked what he was doing when he wasn't going out on dates, and we talked careers for a while. He had a degree in chemistry and was six months from finishing his Doctor of Pharmacy, which I thought was fully righteous. Then he said, "You know, I never figured you for a cop. I would have said, if you were staying in public service, maybe a firefighter. But with that back injury probably not, huh."

"Yeah, no way that was going to be a good idea. I just renewed my EMT certification though. Gotta say, I get a large charge out of that. There is no cruising around, you only go out when there's a reason."

"Well, no law says you can't be a contractor *and* an EMT."

"You make an excellent point, Lieutenant. It's been great talking to you. If we get over to San Diego for your graduation, where's the best place to stay?" He sounded so pleased to give me a recommendation, I knew we'd have to make it happen. "Take care of yourself, Todd."

"You too, Lou." We disconnected and I immediately put the graduation in my calendar. I had the idea June wasn't a bad time for Gloria to take a weekend off. Then I had to take a second to check in with myself, because making plans six months out had not even seemed optimistic, only normal. Well, she was about to move in with me, and she loved me, and why wouldn't we still be good in six months? By then I might even have the balls to propose. This tiny little insecure voice in my head said to mention it to her right now, like somehow I could lock her down. That was obviously bullshit, but on the other hand maybe she needed to know that I was thinking way out in front, so I sent a text: *Hey gorgeous I talked to that guy I told you about, the Iraq leg case. He's got a cool thing in San Diego in June and I told him we'd try to be there. FYI, I also have been advised if I do not introduce you to my parents like yesterday I'm in the doghouse for the next three years minimum*

I got a reply at a time that said 'mid-show break,' and it made me laugh: *Iraq leg case srsly Lou? Does he have a NAME? Haven't been to San Diego for a decade*

76

would love to go. Let's please see your folks before we see mine, mine are a pain in the ass

His name is Todd Sorenson. Find out from Gino when I could run off with you for a weekend in Atlantic City

OMG that's right LOL his mother lives there too she is the cutest. I'll make a scene about how we've never had a vacation, he'll cave in approx 2 seconds. C U at my place?

I'm there right now. Love you baby

Love you too!

It was going to be a really long time before seeing that didn't make my heart seize up. Maybe forever.

Because of the show schedule, Gloria's move was scheduled for the Monday before Christmas. Gino's stage was actually dark on Christmas Eve and Christmas Day. After consultation with her grandma and with my friend the pilot, we'd decided to fly over to Santa Fe and back on Christmas Eve. Gloria claimed that two days to settle in was going to be plenty, and that then having Christmas Day to ourselves at home was going to be perfect. She told me in no uncertain terms that I was not to buy her a present. I frowned at her and told her that was not an acceptable stipulation. She asked why, and I said, "Because you moving in with me is the biggest, best present I've ever gotten in my life."

She bit her lip and gave me this 'aww' look. "But you're taking me to Santa Fe, which is the biggest, best present I've ever gotten in *my* life."

I blinked, because that was hard to argue with. I had, however, already bought her a present, so I needed to win this one. "But I'm taking you so that I can meet

77

your Grandma Ynez, and I don't have any grandmas anymore, so this trip is also a present for myself." She opened her mouth to say something, then closed it again. Apparently I won. To make sure, I kissed her before she could think of a counter-argument, and then we both stopped thinking about trivia like Christmas presents.

I made a point of congratulating her for having so little stuff. Packing the U-Haul took no time. She drove it, and I followed in her car. We left the apartment unlocked so her neighbors could go in and take the furniture they wanted. I was really looking forward to seeing Gloria's face when she saw the house again. She hadn't been out there since the painters got done. There had been some minor bitching (from the painters) about working when it was cold, but the conditions were fine for the paint itself (it wasn't *that* cold) and I overpaid them a little (it was the holidays, after all), and I was reasonably certain the project was a success. I'd sent a few pictures to my parents and Mom sent back a thumbs-up.

When I pulled up beside the little truck in the driveway, Gloria was already standing beside it. She had this fantastic coat on, tan suede with that wavy natural-sheep-fur trim, over a sweater and blue jeans and boots. She hardly ever wore jeans, said she thought they made her ass look too big, so every time she did I made a point of complimenting her ass. I couldn't see it because of the coat. I made a point of complaining about that as I went to stand beside her. She gave me an amused look. "So what do you think?"

"Shouldn't I be asking you that?"

"Lou, plain old white would have been fine with me. I love this color. I couldn't believe you agreed to paint your house purple."

"It's not purple," I said. "It's gray." She snorted. "Okay, kind of lavender-gray. It's twilight." That was what she said when she showed me the paint chip. And she was right: this particular lavender-gray was exactly the color of a desert twilight. It did have a distinctly purple *flavor* to it, but it wasn't grape-soda-flavored purple. And honestly I wouldn't have cared if it were. When she posted a picture, which I knew she would, the internet was going to have a field day. I was going to be called all kinds of names for agreeing to this. Maybe I'd make sure she took the picture with me in uniform in front of the house. Maybe people would think twice about abusing a cop online. "Let's go in and you can see the rest before we start hauling."

"Okay." She put her arm around me as we walked to the front door. I opened it up and we went in. She said, "Oh *yes* baby. You are the most awesome man in the history of men."

I could listen to that all day, especially with her arm around me. "You didn't think I'd do it, did you?"

"I did not. The Rogues are going to give you so much shit. Your cop friends are going to give you so much shit. *Sergei* is going to give you so much shit." She was giggling, leaning on me, gazing across the hot-pink living room. "What the fuck did the painters say?!" She cracked up.

"Something in Spanish about how high was I." She kept laughing. I was grinning. The irony was, I really liked the color. It wasn't bubble-gum pink any more than the outside was grape-soda purple. This was – Gloria had said, and I had agreed – the color of sunset. It was definitely pink, but there was a strong overtone of gold. Not coral, not flamingo, but the pink of a Maxfield Parrish painting. It was warm and energetic, like Gloria herself, and I already knew that when the morning light hit the courtyard the entire space glowed. There was so much stone and wood in the room – floor and ceiling were both clad with oak – that I thought I could live with this for a long time. The kitchen's oak cabinets and soapstone counter didn't fight with it, and it somehow brought out all the variation in the stone of the fireplace. "It looks good with the backsplash, doesn't it?" I couldn't resist pointing that out. The kitchen had been finished for over a year. The backsplash Gonzo and I put in was a mosaic of one-by-two-inch ceramic tiles, in a vertically-oriented running bond. I'd chosen a salt glaze, a little bit speckled and uneven, in shades of gray and tan with flecks of black. We called the effect 'squirrel fur.'

"It looks gorgeous. Oh my God, Lou. It's going to be so nice living here. Did you paint Gonzo's room?"

"No, he looked at your colors and said get out." She laughed again. "Come and see the music room." She must have guessed by now that I'd gone with all her selections, so the calm silvery blue of the music room was no surprise. Then it was back across the living area to the master suite, midnight-blue as specified. She made a happy sound. "We'll get some blackout drapes in here after Christmas. At least I got the hardware up."

"You are the absolute best. I love you so much." She turned and burrowed into my arms.

I kissed the part of her face I could get to. "I love you too."

VI – Gloria

December 2015

I had to let the whole Christmas-present thing go. The truth is, I suck at presents. I always intend to shop, but then I can't think of anything that doesn't seem lame or obvious, and I procrastinate, and it doesn't happen. If Lou thought me moving in was the best possible present, I would simply have to make sure he continued to think so. With that in mind, I went and stocked up on bedroom goodies, packed them into a bright-green basket from the craft store, tied a big bow on the handle with candy-cane-striped ribbon, and hid it in my cargo space.

While I was out shopping I got myself some OTC sleep aids. You would think that a quiet house miles out of town would be easier to sleep in than a noisy city apartment. I figured I would adjust, but those first couple of days I kept waking up. My brain was expecting noise, I guess, and when there wasn't any it freaked out. It wasn't a big deal. We only had those two weeknight shows to do and then the holiday. By the end of that I'd be adjusted.

Christmas Eve was bizarrely fun, up to a point. We bundled up and got to the little airport when it was still barely light. I'd barely slept so I was approximately as good company as a hibernating bear. Lou and his pilot friend had some kind of conversation, we all got onboard, there was a brief delay for whatever, and then we were in the air. It was nothing like the hellish hassle of my previous commercial airline flight experiences. I was still half-asleep when we got to Santa Fe. But Grandma Ynez was right there waiting for us, and she'd brought coffee and churros. "I love you Grandma," I said with my mouth full. Lou and the pilot had some more conversation. I managed to contribute this time, thanking him for such a fast, easy, painless flight. He promised to be ready at 20:00. Grandma put us in her car and took us home.

Lou was perfect, as usual. Respectful, courteous, soft-spoken, funny. He'd brought her a gift. And it was the perfect gift, of course: a new pump for her little waterfall, and a heater to keep the tiny pond from icing up. She and I sat (wrapped in serapes; it was cold) on her tiny patio and watched while he installed them, connecting them to a new heavy-duty outdoor-rated extension cord. She asked me in Spanish when we were getting married. Lou answered, also in Spanish, "As soon as I'm brave enough to ask her."

I did my best to hide the swoon, and said, "His best friend is Mexican, abuelita. His Spanish is almost as good as mine." So then we had to tell stories about Gonzo, and Salma, and how Gonzo helped Lou rebuild that house. We showed her a zillion pictures and answered (or dodged) a zillion questions. We ate pretty much continuously. In the evening, when we were all reluctantly agreeing that Lou and I should stop eating and drinking so we could survive the flight home, Grandma nudged me and said, "So I bet you're sorry now you had your tubes tied."

I knew my face was bright red, and Lou looked like he'd been hit with a baseball bat. He'd never asked me about my method, simply trusted me. My heart lurched suddenly. What if he wanted kids? What if that was a deal-breaker? What if he'd secretly wanted me to get pregnant, so we would 'have to' get married?

What if I was a complete catastrophizing idiot. I had a sip of water, tried to compose my mind, and said what I needed to say. "Actually, I still don't want kids. I agree that Lou is amazing genetic material with amazing paternal potential. But I am a professional musician and always will be. I do not want to rearrange my life to accommodate a child." I moderated my tone because of Grandma's sweet, disappointed face. Lou could have won a poker tournament with his. "I would be a shitty mother, abuelita. I swear all the time, and I drink, and I run around the house naked. I am impatient and self-absorbed and I only cooperate with people I love. I would be such a bad example. Also I'm thirty-six and I'm only now making a decent living."

I could see her think about saying how it wasn't only me anymore, but the rest of it was still true and she knew it. She made a resigned gesture to accompany a frustrated sound, and very kindly did not ask Lou to comment. Somehow we managed to finish out the visit with several categories of frivolous small talk, including some fairly cheerful parent-bashing (my parents, that is, including the one that was her son), and then she took us back to the airport. The pilot was there. We were in the air without delay and on the ground in Clark County by 22:00. It was a very quiet flight. I was getting nervous. "I'm sorry about that," I said as we got into my car. "I hope that didn't ruin things." Ruin today, ruin tomorrow, ruin everything. "I should have told you before." Now I was getting upset. He still wasn't talking.

We were almost home before he said anything. "I owe you a huge apology."

I said, inelegantly, "Eh?"

He patted my thigh. "I was letting that conversation go until we moved in together, and that just happened, but I realize I should have cleared that up long ago. You were taking care of contraception but that doesn't mean I could make assumptions."

I pulled into the driveway and turned off the car. "I shouldn't have either. I assumed I could have what I wanted, which was you, and pretend I didn't need to know any more. How bad did I screw up?"

"You didn't screw up at all." He had his seatbelt off and was turned toward me. "I don't want kids either. If I did, I'd've had some by now." He must have seen the depth of my relief. He leaned over and kissed me. "I was with somebody for a while. She got to be thirty-two and said, you know Lou, I can't wait forever. She wanted to get married. Wanted to have kids. I was still active duty. I said, I'm sorry but this is all I'm good for. So she left, and the next year I got blown up again. I had an hour or two of wishing I was going home to someone. It would have been nice to be taken care of. Even then I thought, that's a shitty way to think of a wife. Someone to take care of me. I went home to Mom instead."

I cleared my throat. "And she took care of you?"

"No, she hired a nurse and ordered a lot of takeout." I couldn't help smiling. He smiled back. "How I want to think of a wife is … the person I always want to be with."

"I like that way of thinking." But I didn't want to force any declarations. And besides, I needed to pee. "Your Christmas present is in the cargo bay." I got out of the car and stood beside it, looking up at that unbeatable star-filled desert sky. I heard the hatch open, and some scuffling. Heard him laugh. Smiled up at the Milky Way and said, "Let's talk about this again in two months."

He said "Okay" and followed me into the house.

Unsurprisingly, we dug into the basket that night. I got him off with my mouth, and he used one of our new toys on me. Then we fell asleep on that fantastic California King bed, and when I woke up he was gone.

At first I assumed he was somewhere in the house, but he was legit gone. Gonzo was with Salma, so I was all alone out there. I found my phone to check for a message and was relieved to find a text: *Sorry honey got called in there's a big mess on the highway and they needed all available hands for traffic control. Be home ASAP. Love you XOX*

I sent back a quick thank-you, then turned on the TV and found the local news. 'Mess' was an understatement. 'Apocalyptic clusterfuck' was more like it. I let that play in the background while I got busy in the kitchen.

Lou probably thought I didn't cook, because I never had. I generally didn't, but I could when I wanted to. And it was Christmas, dammit. I did that shopping at the same time I did the rest. I knew we'd be eating Mexican food all day long at Grandma's so I went with something completely different. Beef into the oven with carrots and onions. Mushrooms and more onions into the big copper-bottomed skillet. Potatoes in the stock pot. Green peas out of the freezer, and a bottle of California Syrah open to breathe. Then I made some spiced chocolate sauce to go with the ice cream and store-bought pound cake. When I paid attention to the TV again it looked as though the clusterfuck was mostly unfucked. Sure enough, my phone pinged: *Heading in to report. Should I pick up McDonalds?* He put a smiley face on that, the smart-ass. I sent back a giving-the-finger emoji plus: *Roast beef waiting. All I need here is a man*

I can bring one of those home XOX

Ride safe XOX. Knowing he was on the way, I went ahead and mashed the potatoes, did some dishes, and then went to get out of my sweatpants and into my Christmas PJs. I knew he would laugh at those. I figured after a lot of hours wrangling traffic, he could use a laugh.

I was finishing my hair and makeup when I heard the motorcycle. Perfect timing. I scooted out to arrange myself on the couch in front of the fireplace. Heard the door open. "Holy cow it smells good in here. Where's my Christmas present?"

"Right here, handsome."

He came through into the living area and broke into this huge smile. "Could you be any cuter?"

"I don't know, Officer Hot Lips. Maybe you should investigate." I fluttered my eyelashes at him.

He laughed, leaned over to kiss me, then stood back again to take in the full effect. My PJs were bright-green flannel with a pornographic Santa-and-Mrs.-Santa cartoon design printed all over. Oh, they were terrible. Every position. All he had on was that traditional red hat and all she had on was a big red bow. It was stuck to various places depending on their position. With all that to look at, it took a minute for Lou to notice my feet, which were in red high-heeled mules with white rabbit-fur balls on the toes. I had a matching red-velvet-and-white-fur fascinator in my hair. The whole getup was ridiculous, but he was laughing, so my work here was done. He kissed me again. "I like this Christmas present."

"I'm sure I'll like mine too. Hungry?"

"So hungry. Were you cooking all day?"

I got off the couch, shaking my head. "If I'm ever cooking all day, it'll be with the Crock Pot. Come on,

86

Mr. Serve and Protect." We didn't have a big dining table, not that we really needed one, so we ate at the kitchen table. Everything met with complete approval from my cop. When we were both unable to eat any more, and the bottle was empty, I said, "Where's my present?"

He gave me an almost embarrassed smile and said, "I need to set it up."

I heaved a put-upon sigh and said, "Well, get busy." I kicked off the mules before starting to clear the table and clean up the kitchen. I resolutely did not watch as he went back and forth to the living room a few times carrying things. There was a very minor amount of commotion out there. He wasn't assembling anything, that was for sure, but there were definitely several components to this present. I was wildly curious. Finally I heard something like 'whew' and said, "Are you ready?"

"Yes ma'am."

"Great." I started the coffee maker, positive that post-present dessert was going to be welcome, and also that I had thoroughly earned it. Then I put my silly shoes back on and sashayed out to the living room. "Lou!!"

VII - Lou

December 2015

I knew she was going to love it. I knew it was not what she was expecting, if she had any expectations at all. And it was so simple. On top of a midcentury-looking sideboard – a thing I'd managed to acquire in between showing her the house and moving her in – was now a high-quality record player. A pair of speakers were arranged nearby. Next to the turntable: three vintage LPs. Elvis Presley, Viva Las Vegas. Frank Sinatra, In the Wee Small Hours. James Bond: 13 Original Themes.

It's a good thing the couch was right there.

I wanted Gloria to love that present, and she really did. After we got done doing what we did on the couch, she started one of the records and then fixed our dessert. We ate in front of the fireplace, listening to Elvis, and I said, "I honestly think this is the best Christmas I've had since I was a kid."

"Ssshh. Elvis."

I laughed into her hair, then took the empty bowl out of her hand and carried both bowls into the kitchen. It was slightly annoying that we both had to work the next day. Mostly because half of my Christmas had gone to that traffic mess. I hadn't even had a chance to check in with my parents or my sister. So I did that, via text, when Frank replaced Elvis on the turntable. Predictably, everyone wanted a detailed report on the moving-in, Santa Fe, and other events of the week. I promised an email later. Then I simply basked in having Gloria there. Knowing she would always be there, and that 'always' might actually mean 'always.' I could wait two months to talk about that again.

Of course, in practice, that meant I immediately started scheming. There were now three big things on the February calendar: the Grammy Awards, Valentine's Day, and Talking About That. Plus I needed to decide what the hell direction my career path was going to take. An EMT gig wouldn't replace my LVPD income. I'd flatly refused to let Gloria pay rent. I told her, "Save it all if you want to. Spend what you want on your music room. Buy us some good steaks from time to time. But the house was my idea and is my responsibility." She must have seen that I was serious, the way I had been when I told her no, she wasn't paying every other time we ate out. She'd argued about that until I said, "I am courting you, Gloria. Let me do that please." You would think nobody ever used that word to her before. But right from the start, I was not willing to let her think I was casual about this. That all I wanted was the occasional drink or dinner or fuck. I might have thought that would be enough, before I kissed her.

I needed to figure out the parent situation, too. Obviously I was closer to mine than she was to hers, emotionally if not geographically. I had no real stake in her family dynamics. I wasn't old-fashioned enough to want her father's blessing. But it would be nice if we all had a civil relationship, because people get old and need help. They'd be a lot more likely to take help when they needed it if we were friendly.

What with all that thinking, and a belly full of good food, and Frank singing soft and low, and getting the all-hands call at the crack of dawn, I fell asleep on the couch. Gloria didn't leave me there. I woke up in the dead of night. The fire had burned down to marshmallow-toasting coals, Gloria was sound asleep beside me, and the fake-fur blanket from the bed was over both of us. She really was perfect. I stayed right where I was and went back to sleep.

We both slept late. I fixed us breakfast, and then we put on coats and hiking shoes (Gloria's were brand new) and went out to stroll the perimeter. It was clear, cold, and nearly silent out there. "The lack of noise is disturbing," she said after a while. "I feel like the whole world can hear us walking."

"If by whole world you mean roadrunners, jackrabbits, and foxes, probably yes."

"Tell me all the different critters you've seen out here." So we talked animals for a while. She knew more about them than I would have expected, which was probably obvious. She gave me a sideways look. "Did you ever see 'Peter and the Wolf'?"

I actually had, but so long ago I really didn't remember it. She told me about it. I got the idea she might be having some kind of new musical inspiration. She asked if I had any plans for the backyard. I kind of laughed. "No. It only seems like a yard because of the mesquite fencing it in. As far as I'm concerned the desert can have it. Do you want to do something there?"

She said, "Well, the front is so pretty," which didn't answer the question.

I nudged her. She made a huffy sound. "You're going to be pretty busy for the next couple months." Was that a reminder that we had a thing to talk about in a couple months? Yes, yes it was. She made an amused sound, which told me she knew exactly what I was up to. I said, "Why don't I give you the website where I found out how to do the front. You can stare out the windows and think about it."

"That works." We walked on. "Jesus, does this ever end?"

I cracked up. A mourning dove flew out of a bush not far away, twittering like an idiot the way they always do. Gloria glared at me. "It's not even two miles around. I usually walk the whole thing in twenty minutes."

"I suppose it's good exercise," she said grudgingly. I almost laughed again. "Better than the treadmill." That sounded like a question.

"Oh, definitely. But don't come out here by yourself till I have a chance to mark it a little better. This isn't much of a path."

She didn't ask how I knew where to go. I'd lived out here for three years, after all. The unobtrusive markers I'd already left wouldn't help her navigate to the next corner. The only landmark, really, was the house. "I could always head over there if I lost the track," she said, pointing back at it. "Maybe you could teach me to see what you're seeing." So I started pointing things out, telling her how I walked it with a Garmin the first few times. She got the hang of it fast, and it distracted her from the horrors of exercise.

"There's a thing they told me," I said as we crunched along beside the road after turning the last corner. "I was all, if I make more water available isn't that a good thing. They said no, sorry. The desert only has so much carrying capacity. If you attract more wildlife than the food supply will support, it's not good. So one small source, and don't put out extra food unless we're talking about a hundred-year snowstorm. Then I was all, but Bambi and Thumper." Gloria laughed, as I intended. "There really shouldn't be deer out here at all. This is pronghorn country."

"Oh my God. I saw a little herd of those in Arizona once. I just about went off the road."

"They're special, aren't they?" We were back at the house. "There. You can tell Gino how I took you on the Bataan Death March." She swatted me, not very hard. Then I had to get ready to go to work.

And there we were, cohabiting, back to the same routine except we came home to each other every day. Gloria alleged that she didn't mind the drive. We both drank less, and ate at home a lot more. Gonzo was making great progress on the music room, and we all got along.

I will admit, I was surprised by how much time Gloria spent on music. They did one show a night Tuesday through Thursday. I had this idea that meant showing up to play at a few minutes before eight. But no. They met up around five most of the time, worked out their set, brushed up any numbers they hadn't done for a while. Then they had a few minutes to get a snack or stretch or whatever before final prep. I did know by now that none of them looked on-stage the way they looked off. It was a matter of enhancement, not change, but it still took time. They had to take care of their instruments, too; tuning up was always part of the first hour. (I was ridiculously turned on by the idea that Gloria could tune a piano.) Then they played for two hours, with a fifteen-minute intermission. By the time they left, it was after 22:30.

Fridays were their latest night. The early show started at seven, and the late show ended at midnight. It made for very quiet Saturday mornings most of the time.

On Saturdays and Sundays the first show was at five, so they got together at three. When you add in the time to research, arrange, and rehearse new material, it was definitely a full-time job. Plus of course they were about to go in to record the new album. They had Scott

Easton coming out for sure; he'd be staying with Sergei and Gino. All five of them would be in the recording studio from noon to eight every Monday, and noon to four every Tuesday and Wednesday in January. Easton would go back to L.A. on Wednesday nights and show up again on Sundays.

My part? Well, to keep quiet about the schedule, make sure we had food, and otherwise be supportive. It was a good test of the relationship, I guess. I could imagine more than one person in Gloria's past probably whined a lot about how he never saw her. She said something to that effect, toward the end of the month. "You are being super cool about this, Lou."

"This what?"

"This never home and when I am I'm glued to the digital, that's what."

I appreciated that my efforts were noticed. "I knew you were a musician, honey. Just like you knew I was a cop."

"My cop," she said, cuddling close. That was a thing I never got tired of. It might be morning or midafternoon or the middle of the night, but we always got our cuddle on. It was almost as good as sex. "This is kind of worst-case scenario. Making a record."

"How's it been going? On schedule?"

"Yeah, we're good. It's twelve tracks, and we laid each one down in an average of two hours." She made eye contact. "Do you want to know?"

"Of course."

"Okay. Just checking. Because you might think, why aren't we done already, but there's more. We got the main layers all done, and now we're working on extra layers with a few extra people. Some backup singers, some guitars, some different percussion. We got a marimba." She sounded so excited I had to smile. "And I'll tell you something else."

"What's that, honey."

"Ruben and Oscar have the worst crush on Scott." I laughed. She was grinning. "After he left the last time they were like, oh em gee could we make a record with him? Meaning the two of them. I was like, why not? He's totally straight, by the way. Still not my type."

"Glad to hear it." I gave that a second. "What's your type?"

She cracked up. "My type is, well, if you were a dog you'd be like a boxer-shepherd mix, I think. And you're my type."

"And this trumpet guy?" I was being all nonchalant. The dude was barely taller than she was (barefoot), but he looked like that.

"He's a cat."

I swear she waited until I had a mouth full of coffee. I almost inhaled it.

VII - Gloria

February 2016

I said it to make Lou laugh, but it was true. Scott was like a cat. He was stealthy and quiet and inscrutable. We'd worked pretty closely for three weeks but I wasn't sure I knew him any better than I did when we started. Aside from figuring out his gender, of course. But God that man could blow a horn. I wasn't at all surprised that the guys wanted to try different things with him. They had to know any record they made would go out with his name and picture plastered all over it, but they were like me. They didn't want to be headliners. All they wanted was a chance to work with great musicians, make a decent living making music, and go home at night.

Gino liked him. I mean genuinely liked him, as a person, not only as a musician. Sergei did too, which wasn't surprising given his affinity for cats. If the album turned out as great as I thought it would, maybe we'd get him back to do the next one. Somehow I was sure there would be a next one. Gino invited him to play with us one Sunday, the last Sunday he was going to be in town, and he did, and it was a great set.

What with all the recording stuff, we didn't have a chance to get to Jersey in January. And the first weekend in February was the Grammys. The more I looked at the schedule the more I was like 'what the fuck,' but Lou came up with a solution. We would go, he said, on the twenty-first. By then I would be over whatever happened at the Grammys, and he would have been flogged through however many extra shifts they loaded him with as punishment for taking any days off. (I was beginning to feel quite hostile to the LVPD.)

So we went to Los Angeles, and we didn't win, but God it was fun anyway. Getting to meet the other nominees who were there, some of whom claimed they had heard our record, and all of whom claimed they were happy to be in our company. Wasn't that nice? We were like a bunch of twelve-year-old boys at a striptease show, though. We were barely housebroken. None of us had been to an awards show before, much less been there because we were nominated. So we could only hope our standard of behavior was acceptable, in case we got asked back sometime.

And when we got back to Las Vegas, my music room was done.

I'd been checking on it daily. I didn't nag Gonzo (or Lou); I didn't mention it at all. I had plenty to do, and so did they. Plus it was a thing I'd lived without for my whole life, so I could surely wait however much longer it took.

Oh my God the music room. When I stepped in and saw it so obviously finished, I turned to Lou and said, "Could I have a minute?" He nodded and stepped out, closing the door behind him, leaving me alone in there. I gazed around, walked around, touched everything. Now I could bring in all my music. Now I could hook up the computer and all the ancillaries and the Yamaha, and work without headphones. Now I could shop for an acoustic piano, the first one I'd ever been able to have in my own home. I was, amazingly, not crying.

All of the wood surfaces were smooth and clean. Stained pale gray and then clear-coated. I thought I'd find a white piano. Or maybe I'd find a nice vintage one and have it refinished to match the room. Go Liberace up in here, and indulge myself. It didn't have to be a concert-quality instrument, after all. I wanted one with some character, one that held its tune, one with a good tone. The one I found for Gino's house was a solid instrument; we both enjoyed using it. He said he liked the feel of the keyboard. It was responsive to a light touch. Mine could be a little stickier.

I went to open the door. Lou was still out there, leaning against the wall, doing something on his phone. He glanced up and smiled. "You like it?"

"I fucking *love* it. I love you. I love Gonzo. I can't wait to find my perfect piano. When is he going to bill me?"

"I'll tell him to get that ready. Would you be willing to post about it? Let people know who did the work for you?"

"Sure, of course. I'll take some pictures with it empty, and then again once I have everything loaded in. Fuck, I wish I could do that right now." But I couldn't. I had to get ready for work. I had to somehow avoid crowing about it in front of Ruben and Oscar.

Fortunately, they were both occupied with a discussion of Valentine's Day, which was imminent. Lorena had to work, so Oscar was off the hook for a dinner out, but on the hook for doing something nice at home. Ruben was acting all smug because he already had that handled. I rolled my eyes and went to talk to Gino. "Guess what? My music room is finished," I said as quietly as I could. Not easy to do when I wanted to squeal.

"And is that your Valentine's Day present?"

"The next five or ten of those, I think."

"So what will Lou's present be." He gave me a slightly wicked sideways glance.

I gave him one back. "Sexual favors, naturally. One from Column A and two from Column B." He snorted, turned the laugh into a cough, and checked the drape of his lapels. They were perfect, of course. The man wore a suit like he was born in it. (I wish I could take the credit for that description, but Sergei came up with it.) He stepped away from the mirror and rolled his neck. I took a look at myself. "Any word from the producer yet?"

"Be patient." He sounded amused. "Don't want to rush the master."

I growled, and fussed with my hair. Maybe in a few years I'd be as chill as Gino. It occurred to me I was already a lot more chill than I was six months ago. Great sex will do that for a girl. I had to be honest with myself, though. It was way more than great sex.

Which is why I didn't simply hand the sexual menu to Lou and tell him his budget. I bought him flowers, a thing I was certain no woman had ever done. Instead of a note saying Happy Valentine's Day, I put in a note that said Yes.

Then, as if to reinforce for both of us that the LVPD was not his forever home, Lou had to work a double on the fourteenth. He didn't get home till nine in the morning on the fifteenth, gave me an exhausted kiss, and went straight to sleep. Fortunately that was a Monday so I didn't have to work. I checked the pantry and zoomed into town for provisions, thinking fairly hateful thoughts about whoever had called in 'sick' so Lou had to work extra. Maybe now he'd make a decision about the next thing. I wasn't going to push him, but I couldn't deny it would be nice if he had a more predictable schedule. The irony of this was not lost on me.

I had everything ready to go for breakfast-for-dinner when he wandered out from the master suite.

Freshly-showered, fully-naked (Gonzo was with Salma again), and bright-eyed. "Hi honey. Thanks for the flowers."

"Hi yourself. You're welcome. I like what you're not wearing."

He laughed silently, blushing a little. God, he was sexy. "So I couldn't help wondering what you were saying yes to."

I walked over to him, giving it some sway. I hadn't dressed up, because I had a feeling I'd be getting naked, possibly even before we ate. So I was in the jeans he said he liked, barefoot, with a black sweatshirt on. It was a nice sweatshirt, mind you. It had a royal flush printed on the front, with rhinestones and shit. "Hmm, what was I saying Yes to. Whaddaya got?"

Trust Lou not to pretend he didn't know what was going on. We hadn't Talked About That. We really didn't need to. "Will you marry me?"

"Yes," I said. Boy, it's a good thing I was barefoot. If I'd been wearing high heels I would have broken an ankle, as fast as he got me over to the couch.

After a while he said, "I really love you."

"I really love you, too."

"I have to work again tonight."

"God *damn* it."

He laughed under his breath. "No kidding." He patted my ass. "Getting chilly up there?"

"Mmm." I groped around on the floor for my sweatshirt. "Do you have time to eat?"

"Yes ma'am."

"Well, good." I finished the process of getting on my feet, took a second to admire him, and located my jeans. "I'll be in the kitchen in a minute. You might want to get dressed." I looked around for my underpants.

He sighed and sat up. "Yeah."

"For the record, I'll still think you're hot when you're not a cop anymore."

"Good to know." He patted my ass again as we went down the hall. He veered off to the master suite, and I dove into the powder room to get myself in putting-on-jeans condition. Twenty minutes later we were sitting down to toaster waffles with crushed strawberries, a cheese omelet, and Spam. Lou gave me a look of such adoration I had to go around the table and kiss him again. "Did I ever say I liked Spam?"

"Lou, every man I've ever known likes Spam. It was a gamble with good odds." I sat down to eat. "Besides, I love Spam. Mom used to make this loco moco kind of deal with it. When I went to Hawaii I had Spam everything." So he asked me when I went there – it was amazing that we hadn't talked about our whole histories yet, but we hadn't – and we talked travel for a little while. He'd been all over as a soldier, and a few places as a private citizen. We agreed to discuss where we might want to go together at a later date. Then he cleaned up the dishes while I made some coffee for him. This was the most domestic I'd been since Christmas Day. He knew better than to think two special occasions equaled a trend. I refrained from bitching (out loud) about him having to work, reminded him to stretch again when he got to the station, kissed him a bunch of times, and watched him go.

Then, atypically, I did not submerge myself in the music room. Instead I found a movie to watch on TV. When Gonzo got back he sat down to watch with me. After the credits rolled he gave me this look. Imagine a really cute Mexican guy, about five foot eight, with this

100

riverboat-gambler mustache. Now imagine an expression that says 'I am mentally twirling my mustache,' and you have Gonzo. He said, "Porque no tienes una sortija?"

I suppressed my natural inclination to die laughing and said, "You might want to ask Lou why I don't have a ring."

"I did!"

I bit the inside of my lip. It did not prevent a giggle from escaping. "He might bring me one when he gets home tomorrow."

"Oh bueno. So listen, I have this idea." He went off on a riff about, basically, Zorro. I was having trouble keeping up at first. Then I started to think I was getting his drift. He knew about the new record. Everyone who knew me did, and by this time Ruben and Oscar were eating at La Cholla all the time too. They knew each other, in other words, and they were chatty. I thought *he is telling me a story for a song cycle.* Now you might think people do this all the time, but in fact nobody in my life had ever done it. I'd been writing music for twenty-five years and it took me that long to come up with one. He was about five minutes into this when it clicked.

I held up my hand and said, "Stop for a second. Stay here. I'll be right back. You want a drink?"

"Sí, okay." He sat obediently on the couch and I went to get a recorder. His eyes got kind of big when I dropped it beside him. I had to do that because I had a shot of sipping tequila for him, and a whisky for me, and I'd been carrying the recorder between my wrists.

So I handed him his glass, clinked mine against it, sat down, and turned on the recorder. "Start over."

"¿Que?"

101

"Come on, start from the beginning." I could already see the title: Thief of Hearts. Not a terribly original title, I'll grant you, but I'll tell you a secret about entertainment: if it sounds familiar, or if it reminds a person of something they liked before, it's more likely to sell. And titles can't be copyrighted. As long as the lyrics and music were original, no problem. I was imagining a Spanish flavor to this, a spectrum from bolero to mariachi. Imagining what a kick Gonzo would get out of having a story credit on the record. Imagining how beautifully Gino could sing it.

Gonzo wound it up with a flourish – honestly, he might as well have said 'Olé!' – and I applauded. As well as I could with a drink in my hand. Then I started to interrogate him about where this story came from. He cracked me up for real when he gave me this insulted look and said, "It's me and Salma! If we were a movie." Which of course made no sense and perfect sense at the same time.

I told him it was great, and we clinked glasses again. Then I looked at the clock and said "Shit" and he almost inhaled the last mouthful of tequila.

For the record, Lou did come home with a ring. He got to the house at around eleven the next morning, and told me he had to wait until the bank opened. Because he had the ring in a safe-deposit box. Because he'd already bought it, a length of time earlier which he declined to specify. It was perfect for a piano player, which was no more than I would have expected at this point. Not a thin band with a solitaire sticking out to flop around and catch on things, but a wider band with a channel of square diamonds all the way around. Not gold, but platinum, because all my other jewelry was silver. I did not ask how many carats. I did not ask how much it cost. I did not cry, at least not until I was on the phone with Grandma after texting her a picture, which was after Lou was asleep so I could maintain the fiction that I was a tough cookie.

The following Sunday night we caught a red-eye after the show, spent all of Monday in Atlantic City, and came back on Tuesday morning. His parents were very sweet about how we didn't win a Grammy. They said 'next time for sure.' They were delighted to hear that I liked Lou's house and that we were engaged. They were exactly how you'd expect them to be, based on Lou. Kind, generous, funny, refreshingly foul-mouthed, and no bullshit.

His mother, five foot six in her high heels, looked up at me (six foot one in mine) and said, "Thank God you're tall. This son of mine looked like Shrek next to his prom date." Which meant I had to see a whole lot of photos going back a whole lot of years. It was the most fun I ever had meeting someone's parents.

Before we headed to the airport we swung by Gino's mom's apartment to drop off a little gift he'd sent with us. It was the official notice of the Grammy nomination, framed, signed by Gino and all of us Rogues. She was so touched. Then she set it tenderly on a shelf and told her yappy little dog to shut up and said, "Can you believe it took that for his moron brother to call him?"

I produced a 'what're you gonna do' gesture and said, "That call meant more to him than any award on Earth. You tell Vito from me, thank you."

VIII - Lou

March 2016

When I looked back later, it seemed that Gloria and I made some significant decisions, and significant life changes, in very little time with very little discussion. All I can say is it was easy. Both of us had history. Both of us knew how we wanted to live, and what we wanted in a partner. Once we agreed that the things we wanted were compatible, I guess neither of us felt like wasting time.

When I asked her about a wedding date, she said, "Gino and Sergei got married one year after they met. I mean exactly one year."

I thought about that for a minute. I knew those two were kind of a benchmark for Gloria, a standard of functional love that she might well measure us against. But she and I met under circumstances that I didn't necessarily want to connect with our wedding anniversary till the end of time. The night we went for that walk, on the other hand, was something I thought I'd always want to remember as a standalone thing. "How about one year from the first time you met me for a drink?"

"I was hoping you'd say that." She leaned over and kissed me. "I guess you have to meet my parents before then." I laughed against her mouth. She kissed me again. God, I loved kissing her. A few minutes later she sat back. "Mmm. It's funny. For two years I didn't leave Las Vegas. And now we're like, Santa Fe! Los Angeles! Atlantic City! San Diego! Oh yes, fucking Phoenix!"

I cracked up. "Will it help if we fuck in Phoenix?"

"It certainly will."

"Did you really not go see them for two years?"

She performed a half-embarrassed sort of wriggle, not quite a shrug, that was slightly distracting given we were in bed and the sheet wasn't pulled all the way up. "I had a good excuse. The job with Gino was a big adjustment."

"Going from three jobs to one." From teaching, and playing in a bar, and doing the occasional recording session.

"Jesus, yes." She slid down, stretching luxuriously. I ran my hand down her front. She rolled over, inviting a back rub. We didn't always have time – or maybe more accurately, didn't always *take* time – to lounge around like this, even on a Monday. More often than not, I had to work. But for once, we both had the day off. So I gave her a back rub. She moaned and groaned and sighed, which not too surprisingly turned me on every bit as much as handling her did. I loved her body. She was not a delicate woman. Not finicky, not inhibited, and not a cinch to manhandle. If she didn't feel like doing something, we did something else, is what I'm saying. I'd never even suggested the back passage with her. I knew I was too big for that to be comfortable, let alone fun. She liked to be played with, though, same as I did. And we had some toys to vary the sexperience. Thinking about that meant, before too long, I was using my mouth on her instead of my hands. Then it was my mouth *and* my hands. I rolled her over and got her off that way. She made some of those porntastic noises. It was such a rush to see her come. To hear it, and taste it. I stretched out on top of her to kiss her. She licked my wet mouth and squirmed against me.

I slid through her, making some noise of my own. "Want me to come on you?"

"Uh-uh. In me. From behind." She gave me a shove and I sat back on my heels, waiting to be sure I understood. "Get that little buzzer going."

Oh. I was grinning as I leaned over to the nightstand. The little buzzer had most recently been in my ass while my cock was in her mouth, and the results had been mind-blowing. That, plus the lube, and then she was on hands and knees for me. I went to work, one hand slicking myself, then between her legs. A light touch, guiding myself, while the little buzzer went in above.

"Holy fuck, yeah," she said. She sounded breathless. I wasn't even all the way in yet.

"Jesus God." I could feel the buzzer. I wasn't going to have to move. I was in, and she was rocking her hips. I had my hand spread across her ass, the buzzer in the notch of my thumb and forefinger. I tried not to move until I heard her breathing change, getting more vocal. Oh God, she was going to come again. I felt light-headed, and realized I was holding my breath. When I filled my lungs she must have heard me over her own sounds.

She pushed back against me, with enough force that I had to engage my thighs. "Fuck me, Lou, give it to me. God, you fucking monster, do it. I want you to come so hard I can taste it, come *on*."

As soon as she started talking I was doing it. Full strokes, not too fast because it felt too good, and I knew at the end I'd lose control. I'd go fast and hard. I had a hand on her hip, watching myself, watching her back flex and hearing her grunting, growling, gasping. "Gloria." I reached around in front to press my fingers against her clit.

"Jesus fucking Christ, yes, God!"

I felt her going over and it snapped my last vestige of control. I had just enough presence of mind to get the buzzer out before I lost it. I was coming when she slid down flat. I went with her, catching myself on one hand. Holding position, eyes closed, breathing fast. Feeling that jubilant pulse slowly reducing in intensity, feeling my balls relax. Feeling my back, which was saying 'you'll pay for this later.' I told it to shut up. I happened to know some stretches that would sort that out. "Okay, honey?"

I used my free hand to gather up Gloria's hair, giving it a loose twist to keep it off her face. She looked drugged. "Uh."

I couldn't help laughing. I slid out of her and collapsed beside her with my arm over her back. "You're amazing."

She swallowed, inhaled, and said, "Says the guy who just made me come twice. Whew."

"We should go for a walk."

"Fuck you."

I knew she would say that. I could hear the smile in her voice, and I was shaking with silent laughter. In a few seconds she would start to laugh, too … yep, there she went. I stroked down to her ass and patted it, almost a spank. "I'll fix you some Spam and eggs if you'll go for a walk with me."

"All right, okay. In a minute."

It was a great day. One in a series of great days. Gonzo was out at some job the way he almost always was, so we could stroll around the house naked. I'd been promised two weeks of second watch, I had a plan made up to install our little water feature on my next full day off, and Gloria loved me. What a fantastic life.

The next day, I almost lost it again.

Las Vegas had its share of crime. All the usual problems any city had, plus the problems that come along with gambling. I don't object to gambling in principle. I'd have to be a total hypocrite, considering the way I spent my last two years of college. The problem is, it's addictive. Any time you have addiction, you get a whole separate avenue for crime. Addiction to illicit sex equals prostitution, up to and including human trafficking. Addiction to drugs equals networks ranging from hospitals and farms to some fairly notorious foreign governments. Addiction to gambling equals everything from shoplifting to the mob.

Anyway, most of the time our department responded to a call it was 'the usual.' But on that Tuesday in March it was a drug bust, with a lot of officers involved. SWAT and a trafficking task force and a real expectation of mayhem, because this was the distributor, not some street dealer selling by the gram out of a backpack.

I won't deny there was a streak of violence in me. A lot of men won't admit to that, because it's politically or socially or culturally incorrect. I didn't have the kind of violence that produces unprovoked aggression. I didn't walk around thinking, I feel like hurting someone. I didn't go around looking for a fight. But when I found myself in the thick of it, I felt this kind of dark joy. I'd seen it in myself early on. Because my father had been in the service, and my mother was – in her way – a warrior, I didn't feel like I had to hide it. I talked to them, and that's why they steered me toward sports, and later toward the armed forces. All this is to say that when we were briefed on this operation I was excited. That lasted right up to the second when the bullets stopped flying. Then I said something along the lines of "Mother fucker," and heard a stampede of tactical-booted feet as I went down.

I didn't quite pass out. I didn't need surgery, beyond a few stitches. The only reason I didn't walk out of the hospital is they wouldn't let me. Something about liability, and oh yes stitches. Two bullets hit my vest, which hurt like a son of a bitch but didn't knock me down. Small caliber, a little too far away. Another one went through my left thigh. They told me I was lucky, which I already knew. They told me I'd be off duty for a month, and on desk duty for another two weeks or until cleared by medical. They didn't tell me 'maybe it's time to call it.' I told myself that when I saw Gloria's face.

This all went down while she was at work. I declined to be admitted (so many waivers to sign), accepted crutches, accepted the loan of an unmarked car. A teammate, the same one who'd brought me some gym clothes to change into, took me back to the station and stowed my motorcycle. Then I drove myself to the casino, taking full advantage of the temporary handicapped-parking permit, and crutched my way to the performance lounge. The reason I went straight there is, I'd sent a text saying I was okay and I'd stop by. If she saw that during the mid-set break she was going to be expecting some kind of story. Gino and the Rogues might be too; we were all pretty tight at this point. If any of them went looking for news they were going to see only that there had been a gunfight and half a dozen police officers were wounded. I didn't want any of them speculating, fearing the worst.

I was still running on adrenaline, plus a hefty shot of some kind of painkiller that preceded the hefty shot of antibiotics. My leg was kind of numb from Lidocaine. In retrospect it was clearly stupid, but at the time I felt like I could handle this. So I showed up, just as they were finishing the set. The security guy outside the lounge recognized me. His eyebrows went up; he didn't usually see me in warm-ups, or on crutches. I said, "Long story," and he waved me in.

Gino spotted me immediately. He finished the song, because he's a pro. Then he shushed the applause, saying, "Thanks. Thank you. Hope you enjoyed the show, and hope to see you all some more. Now I have to say good night because a local hero just walked in and my piano player needs to go talk to him." There was a little more applause amid the commotion of people turning to look at me.

Gloria was already off the stage and moving toward me. She looked like Wonder Woman. I said, "Hi beautiful."

She said, "We need to talk," and kissed me so hard I almost fell over.

VIII - Gloria

March 2016

Of course after seeing Lou's text I spent the rest of the break looking at the news. I knew he wouldn't bullshit me; if he said he was okay, he was okay. 'Okay' might well mean 'somewhat damaged,' though, so I wasn't going to relax until I saw him.

When I said "We need to talk" I wasn't even sure what I wanted to say. We hadn't talked very much about Lou's not-very-well-defined career options. I knew he wanted to work, assumed he needed the income, and hoped he would figure it out before ... well, before something like this happened. Like this, or worse.

I told him to wait, then went back to the green room, where Gino said, "I'm calling your sub in tomorrow. Take Lou home and I'll see you Thursday." I didn't argue. I wouldn't have asked. Gino loves me, I know, even though he's never said so and probably never will.

Anyway I said "Thank you" and got myself ready to go. Went out, spoke briefly to (argued briefly with) my fiancé, and agreed to follow him home. All the way, I was trying to remember if there was food in the house. I'd sort of intended to stop at the supermarket after work.

When we got there we went in – I was watching him like a hawk – and I said, "Are you hungry?"

He looked distinctly more fatigued than he had half an hour ago at the casino. He had to be feeling the effects of the whole day. I knew what post-adrenaline-rush exhaustion felt like, and while I didn't yet know the details of his injury, he obviously had one.

"Starving. Had some Gatorade and a bag of chips at the hospital."

A bag of chips?! "Should have stopped at a drive-through on your way to the casino." *Or said something before we started driving*, I thought irritably. I didn't say it out loud because I knew I wasn't really irritated with him. I was furious and frightened and wishing he had any other job in the world.

No doubt he could read all that. He hitched himself over to the table and sat down cautiously, most of his weight on his right leg. "Yeah, I know. I didn't think of it."

I nodded, because there was nothing to say to that, and opened the fridge. There was not much in there. On the freezer side, there was a stack of Newman's Own pizzas. That would do. I got two of them out, turned on the oven, and went back into the fridge for the sliced ham and shredded Parmesan I'd spotted in there. Pizza tonight scored higher than an omelet in the morning; we could always go out for breakfast. "You want pineapple on this too?"

"Sure. Thanks."

"How about a beer?"

"God, yes."

That made me smile. I retrieved two bottles after dressing up the pizzas. We clinked the bottles together. I drank about half of mine without stopping. He drank all of his. I suppressed a belch, and got him another one. He thanked me and set it on the table. We still weren't talking. I decided it could wait until we were fed. He didn't often drink like that, like he was thirsty for it. Of course, he might simply be thirsty. I got him a glass of water; he drank half of it. Once again I did not say what I was thinking, which this time was 'you need to take better care of yourself.' He was an athlete and he'd been injured before. Plus he was missing a kidney. He knew he needed to hydrate. Therefore, something had distracted him. It might have been the excitement; it might have been the injury. Or it might have been that he wanted to get to me, so I could see for myself he was okay. The oven beeped; I slung the pizzas into it. Closed the oven door, started the timer. Turned to lean against the counter with my arms crossed. "So. Looks like you have some time off."

He cracked up. It sounded slightly hysterical for a few seconds, but by the time he stopped laughing I thought we'd both be all right. He drank some more water and said, "There were close to sixty cops there. Ten percent casualties is unusual."

"The news said nobody was killed. Not even any bad guys?"

"Nope. Our people need to work on their accuracy."

Cold-blooded, but possibly true. I asked a question about the investigation leading up to this, and how they set up the operation. That got him started. He talked until the timer went off. Then we both wolfed down pizza like we hadn't seen food for a week. Between us, there wasn't a shred of Parmesan left. "IHOP for breakfast?"

He laughed again, softly. "Sure."

"Can you shower?"

"I have to keep the dressing dry till after follow-up. Sponge bath for me till then. Want to help?" Of course he would say that with a hopeful look.

"Okay. No funny business," I warned. I did the bare minimum of kitchen clean-up. Went to take off my makeup. Helped him undress. Did not comment on the bruises, or the smears of dried blood on his leg. The big-ass shower was designed as a roll-in, which I'd never really examined before. I told myself it was a marketing thing, because the other full bath – while accessible – wasn't ideal for a wheelchair. Surely he hadn't built this thinking someday he might be in one of those.

But maybe he had. At any rate, he stood up in there and I freshened him up by hand. It was the first time I'd ever put my hands on him that he didn't get an erection. I didn't comment on that, either. In due course we got into bed. He accepted some help, admitting that the leg hurt. Then he seemed to go to sleep almost immediately after I kissed him good night. I did not. I lay there in the dark, thinking dark thoughts.

In the morning, it was very clear that Lou's shot-up leg was very sore. The bruises on his torso were also fairly alarming. He said they didn't really hurt and I said, "Yeah, probably not, compared to that leg." He got into fresh warmups and sneakers, and made a point of making us some coffee to sustain us until we got to IHOP.

Gonzo came out when he smelled the coffee, observed the crutches, and said, "Oh that was you, huh."

"Me and five other guys."

"Everybody okay?"

"Last I heard."

"Está bien." Gonzo gave me a sideways glance. "You going to yell at him?"

I was almost insulted. "No."

"I'll bring home dinner." He waved off our thanks, filled his travel mug, and headed out.

Watching Lou get around on the crutches, I said, "You've done that before, haven't you. What did you break?"

He gave me an amused look. "Fibula. Motorcycle turned over on me. There was a sprained ankle back in the day, too."

The only reason I didn't comment on that was, well, three reasons. I liked the motorcycle, and I knew he loved it, and I'd sprained an ankle myself once. "I'll bet you're hungry again."

"You'd win that bet. I'll start walking on this tomorrow."

That sounded like a warning, and I assumed it meant 'it will look like it hurts, and it will, but that's life.' It was a reminder – as if I needed one – that my man was a soldier. He didn't want me to fuss. Lucky for him fussing is not in my nature. I could, however, ensure that he was packed full of steak and eggs (with hash browns, sausage, biscuits and gravy). I left him in the car to nap while I bought out the supermarket, and did not allow him to carry in so much as a loaf of bread. He made that easy by not waking up until I was almost done. Then I parked him on the couch, gave him the TV remote, and went into my music room.

I wasn't really working on anything. The Gonzo idea was percolating, but I was listening to music for now. Loading my brain with references and themes, phrasing and dynamics, harmonic tricks and orchestration. Once I felt like I had a good understanding of Spanish music (and by Spanish I mean Mexican and South American too) I would stop listening and let it all sit and gel for a while. I wouldn't start writing until I was far enough away from it that I wouldn't inadvertently copy something. So today I listened to music for an hour or so, then played exercises for half an hour. Then I got out a book of Scott Joplin ragtime music, which was both challenging and fun to play, and always put me in a good mood. After that I did my taxes.

I usually leave it until the last minute, but they were so easy to do (now that I had one W2-issuing job) that there was no excuse. The 1099 from the record company was a minor and delightful complication. By the time I was done I figured the man might want a snack. This proved to be the case. I wondered if he was going to wait for me to say 'so about this shitty job of yours,' and if so how long I should wait. I really didn't want to be pushy. It was only Latest Bullet Wound Plus One.

But maybe me keeping my trap shut was the correct approach, because he didn't even wait till Plus Two. In the early evening, a couple hours before we could reasonably expect Gonzo, he said, "I've been thinking."

I did not say anything snarky, which was a concession to the bullet wound. "Ready to talk about it?"

"Well, I think so. There's a thing I never told you before. When I was twenty-one and twenty-two, I was a gambler."

I sat up straight, staring at him. "You?!"

He laughed under his breath. "Yeah. I told you I don't like math. That was a lie. I'm good at it. It's like a game. Did you hear about the college kids who took the casinos for a lot of money? Well, that was me."

I couldn't have been more surprised if he'd said he used to be a woman. "You mean literally you?"

"Not literally. I played by myself. I played in every casino in Atlantic City. Mostly blackjack, but the other games too. I made a lot of money."

"But you spread it out so they didn't send Guido to break your legs." He laughed again. I couldn't get over it. "Is that how you bought the house?"

"That's how."

"I will be damned." I thought for a few seconds. "You made your stake and quit. Why are you telling me this now?"

He sighed and changed position, indicating that he would like to cuddle. That took a bit of maneuvering because of his shot-up thigh, but we figured something out. He kissed me and said, "If I walk into one of the casinos and tell them I want a job, I could get one. A job in security, watching for the people cheating, but also the people who are doing what I did. It's like when the FBI hired Frank Abagnale."

We'd just watched 'Catch Me If You Can.' I raised my eyebrows. "What you did isn't illegal."

"No. But they still want to make sure they aren't getting hit too hard. If I worked in a casino I could have steady hours. Hours like yours. Maybe even the same as yours. It's pretty good money. It's not like the guys who watch the doors. What do you think?"

What I thought was that if he was even asking me, his mind was ninety percent made up. "You probably wouldn't get shot again, would you."

"Mmm, probably not."

"Would you be suicidally bored in a week?"

"I don't think so."

"Then I'm in favor." That was a very mild way of saying it was the greatest idea I'd ever heard. I didn't care if he *was* bored, I only wanted him to never be shot at again. I finally had the man I wanted to have a future with, and frankly I thought a little boredom was a fair

117

exchange for better odds of having a future. Maybe Lou thought so too.

IX - Lou

April 2016

On Gunfight Plus Two I had to concede that my intention of walking without crutches was overly optimistic. The thighbone wasn't damaged; there were no bullet fragments in the wound; the major nerves and blood vessels were intact; but the muscles were severely insulted. I was taking the bare minimum of painkillers, along with antibiotics. The first made me groggy and the second made me queasy. I was not well, in other words, and my housemates knew it.

Neither of them wanted me driving myself into town for a follow-up, especially one that was 'come in whenever and we'll see you when we can.' After a brief discussion, we agreed that Gloria would take me in, and Gonzo would collect me. Neither of them said 'you should not have driven yourself home on Tuesday' but we were all thinking it. At least Gloria had been right behind me.

Anyway, we did that little bit of Kravitz-juggling. The physician assistant removed the dressing and gave me a thorough inspection. The entry wound wasn't quite closed. I asked to see the back and she looked dubious. I said, "You've seen the rest of me, right?" But she hadn't. So I told her to check my history, told her about the field surgery in Afghanistan, and showed her that scar. After that she found me a hand mirror and let me have a look. The exit wound did look kind of bad. The stitches would need to come out in a week or so, she said. She told me there was no sign of infection. I said, "Can I stop taking those antibiotics?" She said no, not until the next follow-up. Then she interrogated me for a while about pain, appetite, sleep, mental state, et cetera. There was even a question about how much time off I was planning to take. I figured that was a question my commander needed an answer to, but not this person. I said I would wait and see.

When she cut me loose, Gonzo was already there waiting. He said Salma had something for me, so we went over to La Cholla. 'Something' turned out to be a catering pan packed with a week's worth of food. Salma came out from behind the counter and hugged me, kissed me on both cheeks, and told me to feel better soon. "I already feel better," I told her. "By the time I finish all your great food, I'll be cured." Then Gonzo took me home. I was asleep long before Gloria got back.

On Friday I did next to nothing. On Saturday I had another follow-up, and felt well enough to handle it on my own. By then I was taking some weight on the leg. The entry and exit were scabbed over. I got the all-clear to discontinue antibiotics and to take a much-needed shower. I also got a pat on the head for recovering. Apparently one of my colleagues wasn't doing so well. I found out he'd been re-admitted for intravenous antibiotic treatment. They wouldn't let me go see him, so I went to the hospital gift shop and sent up the biggest stuffed animal they had.

After that it was a visit to the station to confirm I could hang onto the car for a few more days. I had combined crutches and my motorcycle before, but something told me I might find myself handcuffed to the bed if I got caught trying that nonsense now. For the record, 'handcuffed to the bed' was not in and of itself an unpleasant prospect. It worked great when we tried it before. But Gloria made herself clear: no fun and games until I was off the crutches, or until I passed her personal inspection, whichever came first. She said if it was an arm, we could work around it. That close to the goods, not really.

On Sunday morning I suggested a specific sort of workaround, namely her mouth on me, after she woke up and found me with cock in hand. She said, "What were you thinking about?"

"You. Lying there all pretty and soft and warm."

"Oh." She looked pleased, and also interested. She liked watching me handle myself. "That does look kind of tasty."

My cock jumped in my hand. I rocked my hips a little. If she didn't get her mouth on me I was going to come pretty fast anyway. She put her hand on my good thigh, slid it between my legs, and cupped my balls. "Jesus, Gloria."

"Keep going. I want to see you." She wasn't just watching. That hand was doing things.

"Mmm." Fucking my hand now. I could feel the pull in my injured leg but I didn't care. She shifted closer, her breast pressed against my thigh, and I made some kind of desperate sound. Then her mouth closed over the head of my cock and I went off. She made a sound that might have been 'oh yeah' if her mouth wasn't full. I said "Fuck!" really loud, and then she was laughing. After a few seconds she let go of me and lunged for my mouth. There was a minute of high-intensity kissing. Then she pushed up, and stared at me in a meaningful way. I scooted down. "Get on my face."

She didn't waste any time. "Yes. Oh God. Yes. Lou, you filthy fucker." I had a mouthful of her wet pussy, my thumb up inside her, and my fingers playing behind. She went over almost as fast as I did. While she was catching her breath, I nuzzled her thigh. "Your face is wet."

"How do you think that happened?"

She laughed again and rearranged herself. "You're feeling a lot better."

"Yes I am. I might go for a walk."

"Not the whole perimeter, please, Officer Tough Guy."

"No ma'am."

"And no messing around with the water feature."

"No ma'am."

"Have you talked to your commander?" That sounded neutral. She might have meant several different things.

"I stopped in on Saturday to make sure it was okay to keep the car. Didn't really talk about anything else. I'm going to take this next week and call it vacation. Then I'll ask around at the casinos." She relaxed a little. "Were you thinking I'd change my mind once I was feeling better?"

"It was a possibility."

"Yeah. Well, I didn't. My four-year mark is in a couple of weeks. That's good enough." She settled against my chest; I wrapped an arm over her back. After a while I said, "One of the guys who got hit isn't doing so good."

"Uh-oh. Someone you're close to?"

"No. A guy from the task force, a detective. I'll check in later to see if there's an update." She patted my chest. We got out of bed and on with our day. For me that was breakfast, lying on the couch watching a movie, then another snack, then a short walk. For Gloria it was breakfast, a shower, her stretches, and some time in the music room before she headed into town.

I make it sound like it was this long trip. My land was only fifteen miles north of the Strip. I could have walked it, if I'd needed to. Not, by choice, with a bullet wound in my leg. Up one side of the property and back was plenty on this particular day, though the conditions for walking were ideal.

Gonzo had left before we were out of bed. He often went into town to help at the restaurant on Sundays. I still hadn't mentioned the idea of building another house. I thought there'd be time enough for that after I got settled into a new job. I did a little research online, trying to get a sense of the culture at the different casinos. Then I got on the phone with my parents to let them know how I was doing, and what I was thinking about doing.

Mom was delighted. "Finally! A job where people won't be shooting at you!"

I rolled my eyes so hard she could probably hear it. "In sixteen years I got shot twice." I heard her snort. 'Shot' and 'shot at' were different things.

"Yes, and blown up once. What does Gloria say?"

"She asked me if I thought I'd be bored."

"Do you?" That was Dad.

"I don't think so. I'm not going to take a job where I have to sit and stare at monitors all day."

"Have you met her parents yet?" Mom again.

"We're planning to go this month. They're both in Phoenix."

"Yes, I remember. What about the wedding?"

It figured that would be the next question. I told them what the date would be. Then we had to discuss what kind of wedding, which was mostly Mom telling me how it should be, me saying that was up to Gloria, and Dad snickering. When I finally got off the phone I was more tired than I'd been after my walk. Then I checked my texts because I thought I'd felt the phone vibrate, and there was one from the commander. The detective in the hospital had died from sepsis.

Shit, I thought. Now the whole operation was going to get deconstructed and Monday-morning-quarterbacked even worse than before. If they could identify which bad guy had fired those shots, his charges were going to be enhanced. All the bad guys' charges might be enhanced. It was bad enough to fire on a police officer. To actually kill one was not something law enforcement overlooked, or waved off as unintended consequence, or readily forgave. The fact is, if you fire a gun we assume that you're trying to kill us. We don't appreciate it. All those guys at the warehouse were damn lucky they were taken into custody at the scene. If anyone had gotten away, the manhunt would very likely have been unofficially tagged with 'dead or alive,' which some cops hear as 'shoot on sight.'

I got in touch with a few of my teammates to see if anyone was spearheading the funeral or memorial, the family visits, the follow-up. It sounded like someone else on the task force was taking point. I told everybody to pass my name down the chain, that I could help. Everybody asked how I was doing. I said I'd be fine, that I'd be in to get my bike in a few days. Then I got back on the computer to start putting together a resumé and a cover letter.

It's strange to tell a prospective employer 'I was in the business of beating your systems for a couple of years,' but that's basically what I said. I kept it brief.

Hi, I'm looking to move into gaming enforcement. I've been a cop here in LV. I was an Army officer. I participated in these operations. I studied this in college, and oh by the way I made X dollars winning fair and square against casinos. I have some personal connections in casinos. I'm free to meet any time between now and May first with sufficient notice.

After drafting all that I saved it and read the news for a while. When that got too depressing I went to bed.

IX – Gloria

April 2016

The first quarter of the year was definitely what you would call action-packed. At least I would. Between recording 'Hit Me,' going to the Grammys, getting engaged, and going to Atlantic City, it was already way more than I was used to doing in, say, an entire year. Then Lou got shot, and the next Monday – which seemed like a minute later – there was a sneak-preview party for the new album. The official release date was coming up soon, the same date we dropped the first one. Sergei and Gino did an advance thing at their house. All of us Rogues were there with our partners. Kathy Donovan was invited, with a couple other movers and shakers from 'Behind the Strip.' Among those was one of the stars, a guy named Lucas Gutierrez who was playing a singer with an Elvis tribute show. He was perfectly cast. He looked just right, his voice was outstanding (this I knew because Kathy sneaked some footage to Gino and he showed me), and he was sexy as fuck. It was a good thing I already had Officer Hot Pants in my bed.

Kathy told us they were shooting thirteen episodes from now to June, for release in late summer. Sergei was working a side hustle, running rehearsals for all the song-and-dance numbers. He and Gino had gotten friendly not only with Kathy but with a couple of big shots in the production company, and with a few of Kathy's other sources. One of those had a job much like Sergei's regular gig, except with a Cirque production. She was a retired acrobat herself, and had steered the producers toward casting a Thai aerialist she'd worked with who was temporarily out of a show because of gender reassignment surgery. That person, now a stunningly beautiful girl, was – according to Kathy – a naturally gifted actor who was bringing a lot of depth to the series. "I still can't believe this is happening," she told Gino. "I mean, a year ago, I hadn't even sold the articles, and now this!"

Gino was smiling. "Right material at the right time." He gave me a sideways glance; our record had been like that. We both had our fingers crossed about the new one, 'Hit Me.'

"Jeez, I guess." Kathy gulped some champagne. "Holy God in Heaven."

"What?" Gino and I both looked where Kathy was looking. "Oh good, he made it. Let me introduce you." I watched, not even trying not to laugh, while he towed her over to Scott Easton.

Lou sidled up to me – I had no idea where he'd been, probably flirting with Kelly, the aerialist – and said, "Another conquest for your trumpet player?"

I let him slide an arm around me, though I did not lean on him the way I did when he wasn't recuperating from a bullet wound. He had refused to use his crutches for this. "I honestly have no idea if he ever fucks anybody. Clearly he could fuck whoever he wanted –"

"Whoever?" Lou squeezed me a little.

"Almost whoever. But either he's the most discreet person on planet Earth or he's waiting for Ms. Right. I can't figure him. Oh, here we go, fucking finally!" Gino had started the record. I looked around for a chair or two, didn't see any, and hauled Officer Gimpy over to one of the pool-side loungers instead. We had to sit zig-zag, but we made it work. Everybody else was sitting wherever – there were plenty of towels around – and we all listened. God, it sounded great. The extra time in the studio, and the extra musicians, really added up to something. I almost forgot I wrote it until it stopped and Gino led a round of applause for me.

I was blushing. Gino tried to get me to say something and I waved him off. He rolled his eyes and got Ruben, then Oscar, then Scott to say nice things. I was mortified. Lou had his arm around me and murmured, "You'd better get used to this."

"Gaahh."

He laughed. Kissed my cheek, got me up on my feet, and took me over to Gino for a hug. It was kind of a good night. I talked to Lucas and Kelly for a while. Got into a discussion with Ruben, Oscar, and Scott about this whole 'maybe' thing the guys had going. I personally thought the three of them should definitely make a record, and said so. Several times, with increasing enthusiasm, until Lou took the champagne out of my hand and replaced it with a glass of water. "Party girl."

"Whatever." I sipped water and my head gradually cleared. We were close to Gino and Kathy, who seemed to be talking about something important, but I couldn't quite catch it. Then those people from the production company were in the mix. It all looked too businesslike. Ruben and Oscar were nowhere to be seen. I realized I was leaning on Lou. Straightened up. "Is it time to go?"

"It's getting late," he said, which kind of answered the question. We had to work the next day, after all. Or rather, I did. We found Sergei and thanked him for the party.

On the way through the house we found Scott, on the couch with Sergei's cat Gypsy. I said, "It figures," not very loud, and Lou snorted. "So Mr. Easton, are you going to be out here again anytime soon?"

"I don't know yet." He looked amused.

"It seems like there are at least four people here who want to see you in the near future."

"Oh, well in that case. I thought it was only three." Definitely amused.

I was just far enough away from the champagne to resist launching any nonsense. "Do you have to go back to L.A. tomorrow?"

"Tonight, actually."

"Damn, I was hoping you could play with us again. Well, travel safe, and stay in touch."

"You too." He was on his feet. He gave me a hug, shook Lou's hand, a riddle wrapped in an enigma wrapped in a suit roughly the color of our house. We got out of there, and onto the road home.

Lou had me read his resumé and cover letter the next day. "I'd hire you," I said. "They're not going to do better. And if someone's thinking about doing something shady, having you show up at their table is going to change their mind. What are you wearing for interviews?" I assumed he was going to have some.

"Well, I figured my sport coat for first calls, and my suit for call-backs. How's that sound?"

It seemed reasonable to me, but then I'd never applied for that kind of job. For some reason nobody expected a professional musician to wear a suit outside an actual concert hall. That was one of the things that made Gino (and Scott) so distinctive. With Lou's history in uniforms, the casino brass might be pleasantly surprised if he showed up looking well-tailored. "Sounds like a good plan. I mean, since your suit is not a gangster suit." He laughed, as I intended.

I gave him a kiss and went to get ready for work. That conversation about what to wear had sent my brain off on a wedding tangent. I absolutely didn't want to do a whole white-gown-and-tuxedo thing. Lou's suit was gray, a shade lighter than charcoal, with white pinstripes, single-breasted. He wore it very well. He had a couple of dress shirts with French cuffs. I thought maybe I'd get him a pair of good-luck job-hunting cufflinks. His were nice enough but sort of generic: stainless steel ovals with an etched surface. If he wore that suit at our wedding, maybe he needed a pair for that too. I sent a text to Gino asking for a recommendation on where to shop, and got myself out of the house early so I could do that.

Later, when Gino and I were having our traditional pre-show moment alone, I pulled the two boxes out of my pocket and handed them to him. "What do you think?"

"Interesting choices." I gave him a 'that is not helpful' look. He smiled and handed the boxes back to me. "Which one's which?"

"I thought the sodalite for the wedding. Because it seems like we're going with white metal." Those were round and silver, set with cabochons of polished dark-blue stone. (Yes, okay, something blue.) The second pair were square, gold, enameled in black and red with the four suits.

"Ah. Good call. The others are just right for the job. Is Lou the kind of guy who'll get a playing-card tie?"

"He might be," I said. "Or he might turn into Brad Pitt and run around with his top two buttons undone, showing off his tan." Gino laughed. "Maybe I should get him a spread-collar shirt." Gino shook his head 'no.' I pulled my phone out of my pocket and sent a text: *Hey big guy I was thinking of asking my dressmaker to do one for the wedding. Yes No or ?*

Since he was on vacation, I got a reply before Gino and I went back inside: *Yes. What am I wearing?*

Your suit. You look like a prime minister in it

Better than Justin Trudeau?

Duh yeah you're two whole inches taller

LOL go play some music. I'm going for a walk

Stay away from cactus. Love you

Love you too

Gino very kindly waited for me to finish that nonsense. Then we went inside and got ready to play. I let my sub-brain work on the What Dress Problem during the set. By the time I started home, I knew exactly what I wanted. I thought it was even possible.

After breakfast the next day I went to the music room and talked dresses with Grandma. Then I emailed my dressmaker. It would not take her five months to make the dress, but it might take a minute to find the right fabric and stuff. Most of my dresses were made of printed cotton, the kind quilts are made of. That fabric is available in an infinity of colors and patterns. But for this dress I wanted something luxurious. I wanted – if Lourdes could find it – silk, and I wanted the color of abalone. Nominally gray, but iridescent. Something that would look good with Lou's gray suit but also be Really Obviously Dressed Up. I could wear my black crinoline, and get some kind of sparkly something for my hair. Maybe matching earrings.

No wonder wedding magazines were such big business. We hadn't even talked about the actual ceremony, and here I was mentally designing my trousseau. I hadn't been a bridesmaid since I was twenty-two, and had not seriously contemplated marriage myself at any time since then. I was pretty sure Lou hadn't either.

What the hell were we doing?"

The thought was so surprising that I had to stand up and take a lap around the room. For once, I actually *wanted* to walk. And I wanted to talk to Lou. All these crazy-big life changes were piling up on me and I needed to hear that we were doing the right thing. Or at least that we weren't completely out of our minds.

X – Lou

April 2016

I was happy to go for a walk when Gloria suggested it. She seemed a little preoccupied, and being home, not working, mostly alone meant I didn't have a whole lot to talk about except things that weren't going to be happening for a while yet. So I kept quiet and waited to see if she wanted to talk. Sometimes she didn't. She was used to not talking, even more than I was. A watch in a patrol car might sound very solitary, but between responding to calls, checking in with dispatch, and dealing with whatever law-breaking humanity came my way it was usually not (solitary, that is). Gloria, on the other hand, aside from the hours she was actually at the casino, could be completely alone if she wanted to be. Right up till the day she moved in with me. Because even after she gave me that key, if she'd come home and said 'get out' I would have, and she knew it.

She finally did say something. "I was wondering if we're going too fast."

Oh shit. I did not expect that. I did not like that. I did not know what to say. I eventually settled for, "We don't have to get married this year. Or at all. If you need more time. Or if you don't want to."

"No, I do want to." She stopped walking, so I stopped too. She caught my hand. "I'm sorry, that's not what I meant. I like living with you. I want to marry you. I love you. I'm just having this freak-out moment and maybe it's not even about getting married, there's been so much change and –"

I kissed her. Whatever she was getting at, I needed to kiss her. After a few minutes I let her go. "Gloria. I love you."

"I know you do. Are you sure you're not giving up being a cop for me?"

There it was. That's what she was worried about. I pulled her in again, for a hug this time. "I'm sure. I'm ready for a forty-hour-a-week job. I want to find out what that's like. And the way things are happening for you and Gino, it'll be good for me to be in something steady. Something where, when I want to take you somewhere, we can just go. When you need to take a meeting in L.A., we can go. Being a cop was never my dream job."

Her voice was muffled against my chest. "I know." A pause. "Gino says something's going on with 'Behind the Strip.' Something about our record. We're supposed to hear tomorrow."

"Are they going to use it for the series?"

"Maybe. Something. I don't know."

I set her away a little so I could see her face. Tried to sound exasperated. "Are we going to have to go to the damn Grammys again next year?" She started laughing.

We strolled back to the house, silent again but now relaxed, hand in hand. I wondered what could be happening with Kathy and Gino, if not some intersection of 'Behind the Strip' and 'Hit Me.' I didn't wonder very hard, though. We'd find out tomorrow, and in the meantime we had a few hours before Gloria had to head into town. I invited her to supervise while I laid out some rocks for the water feature. She threw a tiny fit and forbade me to move any rocks until the end of the month. I suggested that I was in need of physical activity, and proposed an alternative to moving rocks. She sighed dramatically and said, "If it means you'll stay away from rocks, fine, get in bed."

Later, I lay there lazily and watched her get dressed. "Does Gino know about your other ink?"

"He's seen my back." She came over to the bed so I could zip her up. I sat up and kissed the sugar skull between her shoulder blades before I did that. The tattoo was by the same artist who did her roses. It had some Polynesian flavor as well as Mexican: garlanded with stylized sea turtles superimposed on palm leaves that looked almost like the 'tribal' tattoos that were so big for a while. Several of her dresses used the same motifs. She had one that was black, with multicolored sugar skulls. One that was ocean-blue, with multicolored turtles. And this one, hot pink with a complex black-and-white geometric border around the hem and on the sleeves.

"You have such a great style," I said, hands on her waist. She wriggled a little. I never could tell if that was pleasure or embarrassment; maybe it was a bit of both. I squeezed her, because a pat on the ass didn't go very far when she had one of those crinolines on, and let go of her. She went to finish her hair. I wondered what her wedding dress would look like. After she left, I wondered how I was going to keep from going stir-crazy while I was off work.

I could still do my upper-body workouts, but I had to be careful about that thigh. A little bit of activity was good; it would help prevent too much inflexible scar tissue from forming. Finding the line between 'enough' and 'too much' was mostly a matter of guesswork. I was spending a record amount of time lounging on the couch, avoiding pressure on the exit wound, laptop awkwardly perched on my knees.

The good thing about that was, I had plenty of time to make sure my job-hunt letters went out to the right people at the right companies, and with no typos. I also had plenty of time to organize the replies that started coming in. This was the first time I'd ever really done a job search. I had no idea if I was doing it right. I guessed I'd find out soon.

We were doing Phoenix much the same way as we did Atlantic City, only with my pal the private pilot providing transportation. The original plan to drive had been jettisoned post-gunfight. Anyway, Bob the pilot was taking us down there Monday morning and bringing us back Tuesday morning. Gloria told her parents where we'd be staying; that I'd been injured; and that we would not be driving around Phoenix trying to rendezvous. I kept my mouth shut while I listened to this. She must have a good historical basis for being a hard-ass. Anyway, we'd be staying put in the hotel, which promised spa massages and a pool (the pictures online made my back say 'aaahh'), and her mom and dad would come to us. Separately. I got the idea they couldn't be in the same room without bloodshed.

I already knew that 'Bartolo' was her father's name, and therefore I was not surprised by Gloria's Samoan mother. She was a substantial woman, with a strong resemblance to her daughter. We got along fine as soon as she figured out that I was not going to put up with any snide comments about Gloria's profession, or about the fact that Gloria wasn't born a boy.

"What the actual fuck," I said after we were back in the room. That was the most exhausting lunch I'd ever had. "All that bullshit about how she didn't have a son. Was she always like that?"

Gloria flopped down on the bed. "Yeah. She and Dad fought about it all the time. She wanted another kid. She wanted a son. It wasn't even a cultural thing, it's just this glitch in her brain. And Dad was like, well, you'll hear about that later. He's got his own glitches."

"How'd you turn out so normal?"

She laughed. "To the extent I'm normal, credit my music teachers. I got a lot of positive feedback there. Want to go down to the pool?"

"God, yes."

Gloria was a strong swimmer, but she was self-conscious about her body. As soon as she got out of the water, she had a cover-up on. I didn't do any of that 'oh you look great' stuff. She knew I thought she looked great. She was afraid everyone else in the world was making whale jokes. For the record, Gloria was not fat. She was tall and solid and fully-fleshed. I floated on the water and watched her get some sun on her legs, feeling so grateful I had her in my life that there weren't even words for it.

Dinner was not quite as exhausting as lunch, but equally confusing. We were at the after-dinner coffee stage before Tommy Bartolo let slip the reason he was a dick to his daughter: he was a frustrated musician. His parents – Grandma Ynez and her husband – couldn't afford to send him to college, so he went into the Army, and his guitar didn't go with him. I didn't see how that was his parents' fault, much less Gloria's. I knew she'd paid her own way through college. So again, we were all civil, but I went back to our room thinking 'what the fuck.'

Gloria read my mind. "They both need therapy."

"A lot of therapy."

"All the therapy. How's your back?"

"Felt great after the pool, kind of tense now. And my hip is locking up." Because I hadn't been stretching properly, because I didn't want to over-stress the healing muscles.

"We could go back to the pool," she suggested.

"We could. And then we could fool around."

"We could. You did promise to fuck me in Phoenix."

"I did." I was smiling. "But I'd better not be thinking about how we're going to do that if we're going to the pool." I was already half-hard. We had not resumed our usual energetic engagements, for the same reason I wasn't properly stretching. The things we were doing were fun, don't get me wrong. But when the words 'fuck me' came out of Gloria's mouth, I got some ideas.

She must have, too. She approached, put her hand on me, and said, "Or I could get you off right now. Then we could go to the pool. And then you could do things to me up here."

All the blood left my brain. "Do things?" I swallowed. Her hand was moving. "What kind of things?"

"I'm sure you'll think of something. You always do."

So she got me off, and then we went to the pool, and I thought of a way to show her a good time. I thought of a different way in the morning, before our massage. And then we had to catch a ride over to the airstrip. Once we were in the plane I said, "Is it normal for them to not congratulate you when you do something great?"

"Totally normal."

Bob heard that. "What did she do that's great?"

"This record she wrote? The title song's going to be used as the theme for a TV series."

"What?! That's awesome! Is it like Hawaii Five-O or Mission: Impossible or what?"

Gloria was cracking up. "Thanks, Bob. It's a song about gambling. The whole record's about a gambler. I'll give you a copy when it comes out."

"The hell you will. I'll buy one. Then I want you to autograph it. Now strap in."

The next day, Gloria got an email from the trumpet guy. She told me about it, offered to let me read it, and said, "You're so awesome" when I said I didn't need to. It seemed he was considering moving to Las Vegas. A long-standing family complication, the thing that had kept him based in L.A. all this time, had been resolved. He couldn't make any moves right away, but moves would be made. Gloria wrote him back. She said she told him Ruben and Oscar definitely still wanted to collaborate and that Kathy Donovan had a crush on him. I gave her a look and she said, "It's true! A very different kind of crush from the one Ruben and Oscar have."

I stifled a laugh and said, "What are the odds he starts working on 'Behind the Strip' too."

"I wouldn't bet against it. That fucking thing is taking over the town." She sounded awfully smug about it.

X - Gloria

May 2016

The trip to Phoenix was good for several reasons. Mostly, I'd been kind of dreading the whole Lou versus parents thing, because I knew what they were like and I knew what he was like. I knew that his first impulse, if they started in on me, was going to be Defend Gloria. And I appreciated that, but at the same time, I didn't really need that. It was similar to the music-room situation. If he'd simply started that rolling without consulting me, I would have been pissed. But in this, as in every other damn thing so far, he was perfect. He let me make my own decisions about whether a battle was worth fighting. All he said to either of my defective parents' unsupportive remarks was "You have to understand I think Gloria is perfect." That is not a thing I could object to.

With that out of the way, and with his job-hunt rolling, and with his clear and present and rapid recovery from Latest Bullet Wound, I was free to get all self-centered and devote myself to my music life. I spent a considerable amount of time with the Yamaha and with my acoustic. I was noodling with melodies and lyrics that might turn into something for the Spanish song cycle. Some of that was done looking out the music-room window, watching a little gray fox who was raising a family in the mesquite hedge across the back of the yard.

On top of that, of course, I had my actual job. That was complicated by my side hustle with Ruben and Oscar. As soon as the 'Behind the Strip' production company had a rough cut of an episode, we were on the hook to deliver incidental music. Each episode was roughly fifty-two minutes long and was broken into five segments. The three middle segments were thirteen minutes long; each focused on one of the five main characters, and each included at least a partial musical number. A song, a dance, a circus-arts performance. It might be a finished on-stage number or a rehearsal or something happening entirely in the character's head. Anyway, so there was a six- to seven-minute segment to kick off the episode and another to wrap it up. We wrote little snippets of music that tied together all the licensed music used in each episode, and that carried in the flavor of our song 'Hit Me' without totally reprising it. It was a fun challenge, and it didn't take all that much time, and golly was it a kick to be on this side of making a TV show.

The thirteen episodes had a fairly complex through-story. It was basically a soap opera, so each of the main characters had Big Drama Moments and Big Emotional Scenes. The thing was full of sex and drugs and conflict as well as performing arts. Once we got the gig, we were given the entire set of scripts. I read them all on a single Monday; I was totally hooked. We had to sign some fairly scary shit about how we would not breathe a word about the plotlines, and would not talk to the media at all about the series story. We were allowed to talk to the media about the music we were doing as long as we kept quiet about the story. This was not easy to do, because of course the music had to help *tell* the fricking story.

Ruben and Oscar dealt with it by saying "Yes we are helping to score the episodes. Okay thanks bye." I dealt with it by refusing to talk to the media unless I was with Kathy or Gino. Kathy was constantly talking to the lawyer people about what she could or could not say. Gino was the face of the music, thanks to 'Hit Me.' He had going on thirty years' experience dealing with the press. Kathy was not shy about telling people he was her inspiration for the (very different) character played by Lucas Gutierrez. He dragged me all over because he very adorably did not want people to forget I wrote that song and everything else on the album.

We worked with a fancy producer from L.A. to remix the track, because neither of us wanted the album version running under the credits for every episode, even if they only made these thirteen. When all else failed in an interview, we could always talk about that. It did not do the album sales any harm. Because of course we had to say that 'Hit Me' was meant to be the first single, but after 'Behind the Strip' licensed it we decided to open with 'Snake Eyes.' And what do you know, everybody wanted to hear 'Snake Eyes.' I mean, *everybody*. It got played on a local morning radio show. The medium-budget video we made was a hit on YouTube. We played it live on the local cable-TV morning talk show. It was moving up the charts within a month, and the casino more-or-less told Gino to add it to our Saturday-night shows, even though it was clearly not a Sinatra song. They said he would have loved it, and they were probably right. I know that sounds conceited. But it *was* the kind of song Sinatra would have loved. The whole record was very Sixties in style, with a mixture of R&B, bossa nova, and big-band flavors. Plus I cannot deny that, all along, I wanted the thing to play like the best movie and TV themes of the era. Big, brassy, muscular. I was really, seriously proud of it, and it was making Gino a star.

He was so goddamned cute about it, it was killing me. "They want me to come to L.A.," he told me toward the end of the month. "I said, you know I'm not a solo act anymore."

"Aw, Gino. You should go. It's such a production for us all to go anywhere. And the guys are still bitching about having to get up so early to do the cable thing."

He laughed under his breath. We were all bitching that day. "Where are you at on 'Behind the Strip'? In good shape?"

"We're up to date," I said. "They're not going to wrap all thirteen till the end of June, though."

"So you're not going to get a break till mid-July, at the earliest." He thought for a minute. "The man upstairs offered to give us two weeks dark this summer."

"He's afraid you're going to take one of those offers you keep getting." I gave him a sideways look. I knew Sergei was a little bit worried about that too. "I say soak them for every bennie you can. We could all use an actual vacation."

"You are so right." He rolled his neck. "I could ask for three weeks. Two in July for vacation, and one in August to do press out of town. So you guys can all participate. What do you think?"

I shook my head. "What if it's not still hot then? I seriously think you should go by yourself next month. Keep flogging it. We don't mind if you use a backing track. Oh hey!"

"What?"

"Maybe you can go on Ellen! She loves music! Maybe those TV-star friends of yours could hook you up with some dancers."

Gino shook his head, but he was smiling. "If you're sure." He knew I spoke for Ruben and Oscar too, in this at least. All of us were very shy around cameras.

"I'm sure. Take Sergei with you. He's been working his ass off too."

"Yeah, okay. You know he'll say, but the rehearsals."

"Whatever. They're almost done. The producers can figure something out. That acrobat lady could run them for a minute. Go be a star." He did something then that he did very rarely. He hugged me, and kissed my cheek. He didn't say anything else, but he didn't have to.

I told Lou that Gino was going to get us two weeks off (because I figured that was a done deal) and he asked if I wanted to go somewhere. I said, "I'm holding out for Cabo in September." That was where we planned to have our honeymoon, a four-day weekend, already booked. "And we'll go to San Diego for Todd's thing. So thank you but I don't think we'll need to dig into your paid time off quite so soon." I fully expected him to have a new job in a matter of weeks.

He gave me a look, because he knew what I was getting at. "You want to spend the whole time in the music room, don't you."

"Yes I do." He laughed and kissed me. I let that happen for a few minutes. Then I put some space between us and said, "I saw the babies again yesterday." The baby foxes, three of them, unbelievably cute. "Is there actually some natural water on this ranch of yours?"

"There might be. I haven't walked every square inch of it. And we've had some rain."

"Yeah, but Mama Fox hasn't constructed a reservoir out there, as far as I can tell. Jeez, it's hard not to start enabling."

He squeezed me again and let me go. "Yes it is. Let Nature do what she does. Want to meet up with Gonzo at La Cholla on Monday?"

"Absolutely. We need to give him some shit about how you're getting married before he is." Lou made a 'maybe' face. "Oh really? Did she say yes, finally?" Gonzo had been courting Salma devotedly for five years. After nearly four years of living with Lou, he had to have a pretty good stake built up. And I knew Salma loved him. Maybe it was a family-blending concern. Salma had a couple of kids with her first husband, and the younger one was about to graduate from high school. The older one had just landed a good casino job and moved into his own apartment. Anyway it seemed like the time should be right.

Maybe it was. Lou said, "I'm hoping so. He seemed awfully excited the other day. I asked him what was up and he wouldn't say."

"Probably doesn't want to jinx it. Well, maybe we'll find out on Monday. God, I want some chile relleno right now. Or chile poblano. Or chilaquiles." Lou was cracking up. I got out of bed to go see what we had in the kitchen. With my work life being so extra crazy, I was contributing next to nothing to the whole 'feeding the people' thing. I will not say it was fortunate that Lou was temporarily at liberty, but it was certainly convenient. And we were all pretty much 'we will eat anything' kind of people, so whatever came home with whoever eventually got eaten. I put together a snack and took it back to bed to share with my man. We fed each other bites and made some representations about what we were going to do when I decided the exit wound looked like a scar and not a still-healing injury. Then we had to do a few of the things we could do now.

The following Monday we got the official news: Salma had consented. There was some legal paperwork to be done, Gonzo confided after she went back behind the counter. They were doing a pre-nup, because of her business and her house and her kids. But he would move in with her at the end of June, and when everything was signed, they would be married. We both sincerely congratulated him. He said, "Without Lou, maybe I couldn't do it. You are mi familia, los dos. I hope you will be there when I marry Salma."

"Of course we will," Lou said, looking almost insulted. "Just like you'd better be there when I marry Gloria."

"Sí, claro. Your parents will come?"

Lou glanced at me. "Mine definitely. Not sure about Gloria's."

Gonzo pitched a fit about that. He knew they were both down in Phoenix. He was threatening to go and throw them in the back of his truck, I was laughing like a hyena, and Lou was sitting there smiling at the pair of us. When I sobered up a little I had another of those moments, recognizing how very right this all felt, and realizing how fast it had all happened. But this time it didn't freak me out. This time I let myself enjoy it.

There were no miracles here, only people who wanted the best for each other, and people willing to work for what they wanted. We all were those people, and we all deserved it. Everything I'd done since I swallowed my panic and walked into the audition for Gino led to this moment. And it was starting to look like I might be within reach of things I thought were only dreams. *What if it were true*, I thought, watching

Lou and Gonzo talk. What if we got nominated again. What if we won. What if 'Behind the Strip' was a hit.

And the funny thing? Even if none of that happened, I still had a sensational life. The best job in the world, and the best man.

XI – Lou

May 2016

It turned out I didn't have time to really get bored. Every single casino I contacted wanted to talk to me. Every single first interview led to a second interview. I rented a car for those, because wearing a suit on a motorcycle is asking for grooming trouble. By the second week of May I had two good offers on the table, and I had to go in to my commander and break the news.

He wasn't very surprised. He said he figured if I was gung ho to come back I would have been trying to get medical clearance faster. He told me he didn't blame me a bit. That with my history of injuries, I'd done enough. Thanked me for my contribution to the department, took my badge, shook my hand, and wished me well.

Now, ironically, I had to get a concealed-carry permit. I was a private citizen again: if I wanted to carry, it wouldn't be on a tactical belt. I got a shoulder holster and spent some time at the range getting used to the new draw technique. Then I talked to Mom and Dad, let them give me advice about the job offers, and took the one I'd already decided to take.

The Friday before I was going to start the new job, when I had my whole new wardrobe figured out (so much shopping, including a nice gold watch to wear with those beautiful cufflinks Gloria gave me), I woke up early. It was still dark. I thought *why did I wake up*, because the house was silent. I decided it was simply new-job excitement, tuned in to Gloria's breath, timed mine to match, and went back to sleep.

After breakfast, maybe because I was thinking about how I was going to have to start living by a schedule in a few days, I remembered that pre-dawn awakening. There was a chance a car had gone by. It was rare, but it did happen. Sometimes people threw trash out on the road. I always cleaned it up. So, since Gloria wouldn't be up for a while, I left her a note and went for a walk. All the way to the main road, and back; moving fast, almost a jog, putting some stress on my legs. I didn't see anything unusual, and I wasn't tired. All I had to do today was go and buy a car, because the new job was a suit job, and I was going on thirty-nine, and it was time. Anyway I kept going, and a hundred yards from where the gravel road started I saw something.

At first I thought it was road kill. That a car did go by, and hit an animal. It happens. I hoped it wasn't Mama Fox. But I got closer, and the thing got to its feet and moved toward me. It was a dog, an Italian greyhound, which is not a kind of dog I'd seen very often. The only time I'd ever seen one, in fact, was in the home of a short-term girlfriend's mother. It had stayed curled on her couch like a cat, at one point pulling an afghan over on top of itself so all you could see was its nose. This one was looking at me as if it wanted me to be someone else. As soon as it was sure I wasn't the right person, its whole demeanor changed. Like for a second, there was almost a wag: is it you? And then: oh. Its whole little body drooped with the same bewildered hopelessness I'd seen too many times in humans. In the child whose only surviving parent was being taken away in handcuffs, or the woman whose promising teenager was being arraigned for shooting someone, or the man whose home was reduced to dusty, smoking rubble.

The dog turned away, as if it wanted to go somewhere. Then it turned back because it clearly didn't know where to go. "Somebody dumped you, huh." About five hours ago now, and the sun was hot. I took my canteen off and squatted down, noting that my thigh didn't object too strongly. I poured some water into the cap and stayed still. "Come get a drink, buddy." After a few seconds, as if trying to decide whether or not it truly had nothing to lose, the dog approached. Looked up at me with the gravest suspicion, then threw caution to the winds and lapped up almost all the water. It hadn't made a sound. It didn't move while I refilled the cap and offered it again. Drank some more. Gave me a look that said 'it's a good start, but humans still suck.' I managed not to laugh because I didn't want to scare it. Capped the canteen, hooked the strap over my head again, and said, "I have to stand up now. Don't be scared. I'm going to pick you up." I put a hand out slowly, touched that thin-coated back. No growl, no snap, no panicked dash away. I stroked it a couple of times, nudged it slightly closer, got my other hand under its ribs. Lifted it. It weighed next to nothing. It didn't struggle. I held it close to my chest while I slowly and somewhat creakily stood up. "Let's go home, buddy."

When I stepped into the house, Gloria was up. She came around the corner from the kitchen saying "That was some walk," then saw the dog. "What is that?"

"This," I said, "is a sound-asleep Italian greyhound that somebody dumped at the end of the pavement."

"Girl or boy?"

"Girl."

"Good. Bare-naked-looking boy dogs are totally embarrassing. It's like, let's get you into some pants." She petted the silky mouse-grey ears while I snickered. The dog didn't stir. "How did you find her?"

"Went out that way because I thought I heard a car around five."

I honestly thought I couldn't love Gloria any more than I already did. Then she said, "What should we call her?" I couldn't even say anything. She glanced up. "Aw, Lou. You didn't think I'd say we couldn't keep her, did you?"

I sort of shrugged. Still couldn't talk. I blinked hard, and she put a hand up to run her thumb under my eyes. It might seem goofy to fall in love with something that fast, but if you've ever had an animal tuck its head in your hand and go to sleep you'll understand. I followed Gloria back to the kitchen. Sat down at the table. Accepted a cup of coffee with my free hand. Eventually said, "I still have to go get a car today, but I guess tomorrow we go to the vet."

"Name, Lou." Gloria was supervising an omelet. I'd put on enough mileage to be hungry again, so I hoped it was big enough for two. "She's almost the same color as those idiotic doves."

I snickered again. "Las palomas."

"We could call her Paloma."

"That's great, yeah." Maybe predictably, Paloma woke up when Gloria set a plate in front of me. I settled her on my lap and told her I'd save her some. I didn't think there was any point in pretending I was going to be strict, but I could at least not set a precedent of feeding her directly from the table. Gloria sat down across from me, stared at the situation, stood up again and went to get her phone. Sat down and took a picture, then turned the phone around to show me. It was completely ridiculous. Plate of food on the table, big slightly-dusty-looking guy with a canteen strap across his chest, and this pointy little dog face with interested ears and bright eyes, whiskers barely two inches from the edge of the plate. "Could you send that to my mom?"

"You bet. I'm going to send it to Grandma too." She set the phone aside and we both ate. Paloma was very patient. We each saved her a few bites, which (after we set the plates on the floor) she ate daintily. Then she sat and licked her whiskers with an expression of approval. "God, she's cute." Paloma turned her head as if realizing they hadn't been properly introduced. "Hi Paloma. I'm Gloria. That's Lou. This is your house now. When you need to go out, say something." Apparently 'out' was a magic word. Paloma didn't say anything, but she looked around as if for a door. Gloria made a comical face at me and stood up to walk to the front entry. "This way to go out, Paloma." I heard the door open. "Yeah, anywhere is fine. Good girl. Wipe your feet. Excellent. Very civilized little princess. Wow, that was some yawn. Are you exhausted? Does Lou need to get you a nice basket to sleep in while he's out buying a car? It's been a hell of a day, huh."

I was completely unsurprised to see Gloria carrying Paloma when she returned to the kitchen. I pushed my chair back. "Guess I'm doing the dishes."

"Yeah, looks like it." She let me kiss her, then went to the living room, still talking to the dog.

Not much later, I had to GTFO. Gloria was due at the casino at five. If I wanted to get done with the car thing and get back before she left, I needed to go. So I tracked her down in the music room, noted that she'd made a nest for Paloma with one of my sweatshirts, and said, "I'll try to get back before you have to leave."

"Take your time," she said. "Get the car you want. If it takes a little longer, I'll send a text to Gonzo and shut the princess in the powder room. She'll be fine."

She did seem to have accepted the situation with amazing equanimity. I petted her ears, kissed Gloria a few times, said "I love you" and headed out.

I'd done some pre-purchase scouting, and I was fairly sure of not only what I was going to buy, but where. The place in question was a Subaru dealership located right next to a Harley-Davidson dealership. It took a little time and a fair chunk of money, but by five o'clock I was heading home in a new Outback, towing my bike. The short detour through a Petco parking lot was good practice with the tow cradle. I walked around both vehicles, confirmed my satisfaction, then went inside to shop for Paloma. It would probably not shock any pet owner to hear that a dog bed was not all I walked out with. It was a whole cartload of stuff. After I transferred it all into the Outback, I took a phone picture and sent it to Gloria with a note: *I feel like such a family man XOX*

She texted back right away, though I didn't see it till I got home: *You're a grown-up now, baby! XOX*

And I realized, as I lounged on the couch with our dog, waiting for Gonzo to get home, that Gloria was absolutely right. I had a house, an SUV, a fiancée, and a pet. I was about to start a new suit-wearing job, and in a few months we'd be married. It was truly mind-blowing to think that a year ago, all I had was the house. Well, and Gonzo. I told Paloma, "Wait till you meet our other human. I sure hope you like carnitas and barbacoa. Tu le gustas? Salma doesn't make it too spicy, I promise." Paloma wiggled into a new position with her chin resting on my chest. "Who would throw you away? You're the cutest." I would never know who or why, and ultimately I didn't care, aside from hoping they never did it again. I was just glad if they were going to throw her away, they did it on my road.

Gloria had given a heads-up to our housemate. As far as I knew, Gonzo never wanted a pet. Of course, as far as I knew, neither did I. Within a half hour of getting home, he was trying to convince Paloma to sit on *his* lap.

XI – Gloria

June 2016

As you might imagine, Lou plus Paloma was approximately the cutest thing ever. It took about a week for her to fully adjust. Anytime the door opened, she went on alert, and then there was this moment of disappointment. We could tell she was still hoping those Other Humans would come back to get her. But her behavior as a house guest was impeccable, and before long it was plain to see that she'd decided this was an okay situation.

When Lou took her to the vet, they scanned her for a microchip and didn't find one. She hadn't been spayed, either, so that went on the to-do list. They were glad to hear that she was going to live indoors – Lou said the words 'coyote bait' were spoken – and suggested a time, a couple months after de-sexing, to get her vaccinated.

I had to take a Sunday off in order to make the San Diego trip. Bob got us there and back. I was getting totally spoiled with this whole private-flight deal. After the graduation ceremony, we had dinner with Lou's friend Todd and the lady he appeared to be dating, who was also a pilot. We talked about her on the way home Monday and it turned out Bob and his wife knew her. Lou said he'd pass that on to Todd, maybe the six of us could get together sometime. It all felt very adult.

I was still working my ass off. Gino made some media appearances, which kept the new record moving. I told Ruben and Oscar that Scott had been in touch and they immediately started scheming. I didn't know when (or if, really) he meant to come back out. Whatever was happening sounded complicated, so I mostly just kept an eye on his social media for clues. He texted from time to time. I always wrote back.

Meanwhile, Lou was settling into his new gig. He was working Tuesday through Saturday, one to ten p.m. That schedule was great, from my point of view. We always had Mondays off together (which meant, until the Rogues and I were done with 'Behind the Strip,' Monday nights), so we always went to La Cholla for dinner. Lou took his motorcycle out for a run on Sundays, a run that usually included a trip to the range to meet up with a cop friend or two and get some practice. He seemed to think it was a good routine. In any case, he showed no sign of missing the cop life.

We were both very aware of the Gonzo Countdown. It was going to be a little strange when he moved out. It wasn't so much that we constantly did things together, but you know how it is. You get used to a situation. It was comfortable. Even though Lou and I now had a lot more regular overlap of waking hours, we were both going to miss Gonzo.

Amazingly, it was Lou's idea to invite Scott to stay with us. When I got another email, along the lines of 'the end is in sight,' I told Lou that the trumpet guy might be rolling in soon, and he said, "We'll have that spare room."

I know my face said 'what the fuck.' Lou snorted a laugh into his coffee. I said, "Seriously?"

"Well, you said he's a cat." I cracked up. Lou swallowed a mouthful of coffee. Then he said, "If the money situation is the way you think, he'll want to buy something. Or build something. But why rent somewhere for however long it takes to do that, when we have space?"

"Gino would probably offer," I pointed out.

"Yeah, but the trumpet. Poor Sergei."

156

I laughed again. "Should we open up the walls in Gonzo's room and pack in some more soundproofing?"

"Sure. We could do that." A pause for more coffee. "I'm guessing this cat doesn't know how to do that."

I shook my head. "And I'm not learning. These hands do not touch handyman tools." I swear I could see Lou thinking 'you touch this handyman's tool all the time' but he managed not to say it. I said it later.

We didn't mention the Scott thing to Gonzo, because for one thing it might not happen at all and for another we didn't want him to feel like he was replaceable, because he wasn't. And I thought I should wait until Scott said something about finding a place to stay before I extended the offer. He might well prefer to handle that all on his own. I didn't even know where he lived in L.A., only that he wasn't very attached to it.

Besides, I had too much else going on. We were going to shoot another video, for the next single from 'Hit Me,' as soon as the Rogues and I got done scoring the last two episodes of 'Behind the Strip.' Plus I was starting to hear things for the next song cycle. I was past noodling now; I had a chart for the part of the story told by each song, what type of songs they were, and some lyrical notes. I could not wait for those two weeks of vacation. There was a good chance I wouldn't even leave the house.

Gino knew something was up. I had – with a titanic effort – managed not to hint at what was brewing in my head. Maybe he thought it was all domestic excitement: Gonzo, Paloma, the upcoming weddings. Anyway, I continued to keep my trap shut because I wanted him to get out of town with Sergei (they were going to New York for family visits and a Broadway binge) with nothing on his mind but his husband.

157

With all that piling up you would think I'd want our regular gig to be business as usual. We're all open to a little improv, though. The last week of production on the TV thing there was a distinctly 'party time, excellent' atmosphere, which washed over onto us because of the Kathy-Gino connection. 'Behind the Strip' cast members tended to go out together in groups. Some of them showed up in our performance lounge on that last week, and there was some borderline-heckling nonsense between them and us because we all knew each other at this point.

Gino was next best thing to cracking up. He put on this exasperated face – this was a Thursday, mind you, not a Sunday night when things tended to be a little loose – and said, "Fine. You punks think you can do better, come on up here." Then of course there was some bullshit about oh, I don't have my bass, I don't have my axe, whatever. Ruben started making chicken noises. Oscar and I were busting a gut. The audience was like, what in the hell is happening.

Finally one of these characters, a woman named Nancy who played electric bass, came up on stage. She said a few words to Oscar. He said, "Yeah, I know that."

Then she asked me if I knew 'Walk of Shame' by Charmagne Tripp, and I almost fell off the bench laughing. The recording by Eight to the Bar was one of my absolute all-time favorites. It was not a song I did with Gino, but yes I knew it. I said, "Who's going to sing it?" She pointed out in the house, at Lucas. He made an 'oh hell no' face.

Gino said, "Come on up, Mr. Gutierrez. You've been called out. Folks, this is Lucas Gutierrez. He's been in town the past few months making a TV show. You may have heard something about it, it's called 'Behind the Strip.'" There was some applause. The TV production company had been releasing rehearsal videos here and there, and soundstage tours were a hot ticket. The guy with Lucas gave him a shove and he started toward the stage, pretending to drag his feet. The other guy came too.

I mentioned that Lucas played a character with an Elvis tribute show, and that he had a great voice, and that he was sexy as fuck. He was Gino's height, long-legged and broad-chested, and you could feel this flutter in the audience. He was wearing jeans and a white tee shirt under a black leather jacket, and damn if he didn't look like the hot Mexican version of Elvis. The audience knew they were in for some kind of treat. Nancy said another thing to Oscar, told me what key, slapped Lucas on the ass, and went over by Ruben with the other guy. I started to play.

Oh my God, it was fun. Gino handed his mic to Lucas and stepped offstage behind me. I could hear him laughing as Lucas went into the first chorus.

Nancy and the other guy were singing backup, Ruben was kicking it, Oscar was having a blast. We all were. I seriously hoped someone was doing a phone video. It was against the rules, but this whole thing was off the highway. The audience loved it.

When Gino came on to take back his mic I saw him sliding his phone into his pocket. He said something to Lucas, smiling, then (into the mic) said, "Get off my stage. Thank you. Folks, that was Nancy and Derek and some other guy from 'Behind the Strip.' Please direct any complaints to the casino management. Now let's get back in the groove. Actually, Nancy, hang back a second." He turned around and said to us Rogues, "Something Stupid?" Which of course is a Sinatra song, and we played it often, though not as a duet. We all nodded; Gino raised his eyebrows at Nancy and she nodded (she did look slightly terrified); and then we started to play again. After the first couple of lines, Nancy had it. I couldn't stop grinning.

The next day, Gino sent us all the phone video he took from offstage, with a note saying the management gave him permission to post it. When we reconvened for the Friday early show, we all took a few minutes to giggle over the comments (and text the link to friends). Then we settled down to iron out our playlists for the night and do some quick rehearsal. The early show, seven to nine, was the same sort of set as our Tuesday-through-Thursday shows: all Sinatra classics up through the Capitol years. Our Friday late show, ten to midnight, featured later material, big ballads, and some Rat Pack style. Gino did some of the songs Dean Martin and Sammy Davis Jr. were known for, with occasionally an Elvis number or two. This time he opened the second half by saying, "Last night we got stage-bombed by some TV people, so now I'm going for a little payback. This is a song made famous by Elvis Presley, but Mr. Sinatra recorded it too. I think you'll all recognize it. Throw your mittens around your kittens and let's go." I played a brief cadenza, Oscar put down some bluesy notes, Ruben laid a brush on the snare, and Gino sang 'Love Me Tender.' Did the audience go wild? Yes, yes it did. The whole back half of the set was on fire. We played three more Elvis songs. Gino didn't sing them like Elvis, or like Frank. He sang them the way he sang 'Hit Me.'

I was wishing Lou was there; hoping, in fact, because I'd sent him a text before we went on. The casino turned a blind eye to him walking in, same as they did for Sergei or Lorena or Carla. It wasn't so often that it would bite into profit, and it kept us happy. With our album still on the charts (and 'Snake Eyes' a bona fide hit) keeping us happy was of interest. God, I couldn't wait to start on the Spanish album. I was thinking about that as we took our bows and left the stage. Then there was Lou, in one of his Here To Count Your Cards suits, looking fine. I kept walking, right into his arms. "Were you here at the start of part two?" I said after a few minutes.

"Sure was. Would he sing that at our wedding?"

"Oh Jesus Lou." I had to do a little blink, sniff, swallow maneuver. If Gino sang that for us I was going to bawl. "I'll bet he would."

"I'll put a bandanna in every pocket."

"So will I." I kissed him again. "Hungry?"

"Starving." He put his arm around me and we went down to the green room to say good night to the guys first. He said something to Gino that ended in a hug.

XII – Lou

June 2016

Gloria thought I was being excessively civic-minded, and I hated to think we might lose Paloma, but I checked with the LVPD and the animal shelter anyway. I wanted to be sure she hadn't been stolen, or wasn't being searched for by a loving owner. I doubted that was the case, because of the no-microchip, no-spaying situation. Much to our relief, there were no reports or bulletins. The people at the animal shelter thanked me for rescuing her. "That's the worst," said the administrator there. "Someone who dumps an animal like that is the worst. That's like, you want this animal to die and you're not willing to admit it to yourself. Where's the nearest house after yours?"

"A few miles," I said. "I don't think the dog even tried to go anywhere. She is not very outdoorsy." That made the administrator laugh, and it seemed like she needed a laugh, so I said thank you and shook her hand, and got out of there on a good note.

With that off my mind, I was ready to dive into the new job. The first two weeks were orientation and training, which included exhaustive briefings on all the games and devices. Most of my personal experience was with face-to-face games, and I hadn't used any of the latest electronics. That part was fun, I can't deny. Then we got into all the ways the casino knew of people cheating. That part was enough to make a person lose their faith in humanity, or it would have been if I hadn't spent four years on the police force. I already knew how shitty people could be. It was fascinating, though. All the countermeasures, including people like me out on the floor, were fascinating too. There was a very fine line between making people think they would get a fair game – even though gamblers know in their hearts that the house always wins – and making them feel like someone was breathing down their neck the whole time. If the gaming experience was not fun, people would stop, end of story. Losing could still be fun. It was part of our job to *make* losing fun, because that's how we won.

It is a bizarre way to look at the world. But people like to gamble.

So that first month was a real change, not only from being off work but from being a cop. I seriously enjoyed being dressed well. I liked the hours, and most of the people I worked with, and the fact that once I left the casino I was done. Nobody was going to call me in for an extra shift, nobody was going to expect me to stay an extra hour writing up reports, and nobody was going to shoot at me. Well, I guessed it was too soon to say that was a sure thing, but the number of guns fired inside casinos was a lot lower than the number of guns fired outside.

I'd been in touch with my buddy Todd over in San Diego, to confirm we would be there for his graduation. I hadn't told him about my new gig. It was great having that to talk about when we went to dinner after the ceremony. Todd had a few job offers to choose from, all in SoCal. His lady Mai said it didn't matter to her which one he took; she could get her hands on a plane pretty easily. They both got a kick out of everything happening for Gloria, and when we mentioned getting married they both asked if they could come. I was more than okay with that. I gave Todd an 'are you gonna' kind of look and he gave me one back that said 'maybe.'

Then it turned out my pilot pal Bob knew Mai, and suddenly my social life was a Thing. Being with Gloria had already expanded my world, and now I had some more people of my own. I hadn't really bonded with anyone on the force, and the other job was still too new. This was more stuff to add to the 'grown-up' side of the ledger, though: having friends outside of work. I'd made a good start with Gonzo, at least.

Gloria said as much when we got home from that trip. "You're good at this friends thing, Lou. I don't know many guys who would have done what you did with Gonzo. Did any of your cop buddies give you any crap about it?"

I knew exactly what she meant. "Oh, sure. Called him my boyfriend. Hey Kravitz, how's your boyfriend. I was always like, well, he's re-building my kitchen today, how's yours?" Gloria laughed. "Nobody was super obnoxious about it. Especially since I started going out with you."

"I am pretty far along the spectrum from Gonzo," she agreed.

"All woman, and no mistake." That seemed like a good cue to get my hands on my woman, so I did. We were back in action with all cylinders firing, making up for those workaround weeks. I won't say 'at every opportunity,' but it's fair to say we'd missed having all of each other. The fact that my new work schedule meshed so neatly with hers helped too. We were going to bed together and waking up at the same time every day. It was amazingly great.

I got off work at a time that would let me see the back half of Gino's Friday late show, and decided to make that a regular thing. The last full week of the month happened to be the week 'Behind the Strip' wrapped production. Gloria told me some of those people hijacked Gino's show on Thursday and that he was planning a little something for the next late show. So obviously, I was there, and got knocked out all over again by how good these guys were. It's easy to get used to something, to stop appreciating it quite so consciously. I knew the Desert Rogues were a really solid combo, and I knew Gino was a really gifted performer. But I mostly heard him in Sinatra mode, so hearing him do Elvis songs, his own way, was like hearing him for the first time. And I knew how much Gloria and the guys contributed. I knew she could do just about anything on the piano. She was in the zone that night. Instead of sending a text along the lines of great show, see you at home, I went a little way down the corridor leading to the green room. The casino security let us – me and Sergei, Lorena and Carla – do that, a major perk of being connected to one of the performers. So I was a few feet away when Gloria came offstage, and she came straight to me. There were a few kisses and a few words, and then we moseyed down to the green room. I went to ask Gino if he would sing 'Love Me Tender' for us at the wedding. He said he would. He looked as though he was happy to be asked. We'd gotten friendly in the past nine months, but this was a step beyond that. We both seemed to know it. "I don't know if you know how Gloria feels about you," I said, quietly, so nobody could overhear.

"I've got an idea it's roughly the way I feel about her." He was smiling. "For the record, I'm glad she's marrying you."

"Thanks, Gino. For the record, I'm glad she's working with you." I think I made the move first, opening up for a hug. An actual hug, like a big-brother hug or a best-friend hug. Almost a Dad hug, even though Gino was barely eleven years older than me. It felt really nice. When we let go we were both kind of laughing, the way you do when something is more meaningful than you expected. Then I went to collect Gloria and see about some dinner.

Over the course of the next week, Gonzo gradually moved out. When he left in the morning, it was always early, way before we were up. He'd take something or other over to Salma's house, then go on to his day's work. He was always in bed before we got home. Basically the only time we saw him was Sunday, when we were having our breakfast and he was on his way to Salma's, and Monday night at La Cholla. He didn't have a lot of stuff aside from his tools. A couple of his contractor buddies came over on the thirtieth and helped him get everything that was left. I was glad I had a chance to shake all their hands. And I was really glad I'd be seeing Gonzo on Monday as usual. "It is going to be super strange," I told him.

"You have so much space in the garage now." I could tell he was a little emotional too. But we were guys, so he said, "See you Monday," and got in his truck. When I went back inside, I caught Gloria blowing her nose.

"Shut up," she said. "This is the longest I've lived with anybody for ten years." I knew about that, of course. I was planning to celebrate, in some small way, each year we marked off. When I was officially her longest-lasting cohabitator, there was going to be a party.

"Good thing he's only across town," was all I said. "What have you heard from the trumpet guy?" I always called him that, and Gloria always rolled her eyes. No exception today.

"Nothing firm. There was some kind of snafu with selling the house."

"So I guess we have a little breathing room."

She moved in on me for a hug. "No need to bust open the walls yet. Actually, no reason to do it at all. You know if he ends up crashing here for a while, he can practice when we're at work."

It was so nice to hold her. To hold Gloria, specifically, not simply 'a woman.' I'd already told her how great that show was the week before. Told her every day that I loved her and her music. Couldn't wait to see – or hear – what she did next. "So when are you going to tell Gino about whatever you've been cooking up lately?"

She pulled away enough to look at me, giving me this fake-mystified expression. "What are you talking about?"

"Ma'am, you can answer the question now or we can break out the handcuffs."

She cracked up. "Oh my God, did you keep those?!"

"Hell yeah I kept those. I paid for 'em. They're mine." They were in the drawer of my nightstand. The other toys were on her side. I squeezed her again, a hint that she hadn't answered the question.

"Mmmph. Okay, all right. I'm working on a new song cycle. It was this story that Gonzo told me way back, Jesus, Valentine's Day? When you had to go in the next day? Anyway it was bananas and I've been fiddling with it ever since, but I didn't want to really do anything till we get the TV show squared away. Plus I want to make sure Gino is all Sergei all the time for their vacation."

"Things got a little busy for him, the way 'Snake Eyes' hit," I said. "He's gone as soon as you get that second video done, right?"

"Right. So I can't decide if I'm hoping the TV thing is done now, or if they'll do more. We don't even know when they're planning to release these episodes."

"Worry about it when it happens," I suggested, and patted her ass. "I'd better start getting ready." She kissed me a couple of times. We ended up showering together. When I left for work I was in a really good mood.

XII – Gloria

July 2016

We thought having the house to ourselves was going to be a little strange for a while. The funny thing was, we saw almost as much of Gonzo after he moved out as we did before. Our Monday night rendezvous at La Cholla was such a fixture that the only reason anyone would miss it was an unavoidable work commitment. And strangely enough Gonzo, previously the most likely person to have such a conflict, never seemed to have them anymore. Lou and I decided he'd been letting the workday run over because he never spent Monday nights with Salma. Now that he did, clearly he was downing tools on more of a regular schedule.

So that was Gonzo squared away. They were planning their wedding. Lou was also squared away – he was digging into the new gig, and I thought he liked it – and our wedding was pretty much planned already. We were going to do it the super easy way: in the chapel at the casino where I worked. Obviously we could just as easily have done it in the casino where *he* worked. But I'd been with mine longer, and they offered us a really sweet deal. We made that reservation, told the parents, told our friends, and that was that. Cabo was locked down, and all I had to worry about was my dress. That meant I basically had nothing to worry about.

Meanwhile we were enjoying having the house to ourselves because it was summer, and while we did have air conditioning, we could now run it less and simply run around the house naked (or next best thing). I did not mention this to anybody, not even my female friends. I had a lot more of those now, thanks to the TV show. For all I knew they were nudists too, but I don't think friends need to know *everything* about each other.

What with Mama Fox and her family in the backyard, I never did contact the native-plants people about what I should do out there. Frankly, I was too busy anyway. As soon as those last few episodes were scored, we got into one of Carbon 13's soundstages to shoot the video for the next single from 'Hit Me.' It was the first love song on the album, and we thought it stood a good chance of being almost as much of a hit as 'Snake Eyes.' As soon as that was wrapped, Gino and Sergei took off for New York.

That gave me two solid weeks with nothing to do but take all my notes and ideas and random phrases of music, and turn them into a dozen more-or-less-complete songs. A few years back the very idea would have sent me into a panic. But after thirty solid months of working up arrangements, half a dozen stand-alone songs, 'Hit Me,' and the scoring experience, apparently I was a professional songwriter.

I took it one song per day, from beginning to end, in order from the opening track to the last one. First there was an hour or two spent hammering out a lyric. It had to serve the overall story and it had to fit the right style parameters. Then I took a break. Not a walk – it was summer in the desert – but a break to stretch, commune with Paloma, catch up on email, or whatever. Also, at regular intervals, to go and procure food.

I had to be more mindful about that now that we didn't have Gonzo bringing home goodies from La Cholla all the time. Later in the day I banged out the melody for the new lyric. Most of the time my music brain was working the way it should, meaning once I had the lyric I could hear the melody. I played them straight into the software, tweaking as needed, adding structure with a chord here and a bass line there.

Now obviously this was bass for the piano, not for Oscar. He would add his own stuff. I'm talking about what the left hand does on the keyboard while the right hand makes the melody happen in the treble clef. I didn't try to perfect any of the songs. That would happen when the guys got involved. What I was shooting for was a twelve-track demo that told the story, with a satisfactory progression through distinct flavors, or colors, or however you wanted to think of the difference between a cha-cha and a bolero. This was going to be a very danceable album.

And even though it was a very Latin album, all the lyrics were in English. This was a Gino record, and we figured his fans bought mostly English-language stuff. If some Latin cover artists wanted to pick up a few of them later that was fine with me. Maybe the one who did 'What If It Were True' would be interested.

Anyway, I got it done, and because of my new and wonderful circumstances it hardly even felt like work. Only once did Lou get home to find me still in the music room, cursing because my lyric wasn't working with my melody, or vice versa. Every other night I was on the couch with Paloma, watching a movie, on vacation. It was awesome. Plus of course we were waking up together every day, and he was fully (I do mean *fully*) recovered from Latest Bullet Wound.

On the thirteenth day, when I hardly knew what to do with myself because the hard work was done and I wanted to leave it alone for a minute, Lou suggested I should hop over to Santa Fe to see Grandma. "I can't go with you this time," he said, "but would that be fun? You could stay overnight, come back tomorrow. She'd like that, wouldn't she?"

171

I stared at him for a few seconds, wondering how he was so damn good at this family thing. "She would love that. I would love that. You realize we're going to talk about you the entire time." He snickered. I kissed him a bunch of times. Then I got online and booked a flight on Southwest because this was too short notice to try and wheedle more air time out of Bob. Then I sent Grandma a text to tell her I was on my way. Lou said he would take me to McCarran and then take himself out for breakfast. From suggestion to walking into the airport was less than three hours. It felt so daringly spontaneous.

When I arrived at the gate it wasn't time to board, so I got my phone out again. Grandma had sent me a text back saying *Tu padre está aquí!* I assumed he was there for a quick visit, wondered who was going to sleep where, and then dismissed that as a problem to be solved later. I had another email from my trumpet-playing friend Scott; he was still tied up in L.A., and not in a fun way. Then there was a text from Kathy to say she'd been over to Los Angeles to meet her new lawyer; she'd seen Lucas Gutierrez while she was there. Kathy didn't know yet what, if anything, was going to happen with 'Behind the Strip.' The first thirteen episodes were targeted for release in September. I was fairly sure I had plenty of other things to do if that was all they ever made. With 'Hit Me' as the theme song, I'd make a buck or two till the end of time as long as people kept watching. Music royalties were probably not going to make me rich, but if we made a new album every year or so, and if the albums did well, I would eventually have a nice little stream of supplemental income.

I hoped Gino would like what I was doing this year. I knew the whole Sinatra thing was, for him, a case of 'if you can't beat 'em, join 'em.' Meaning I knew he wanted more out of his musical life than to be a tribute artist. I thought changing it up would make him happy. It was a gamble, though. He was a dozen years older than me and it was not unreasonable that he might want to play it safe. Not a question I could answer by thinking about it, so I dismissed that too and sent a few naughty texts to Lou. He wasn't due at work yet. I figured I'd make him sorry I wasn't going to be home that night, and extra happy to see me when I got back.

The flight was uneventful. Dad sent a text to say he'd pick me up, so I pinged him as soon as we landed. We'd have plenty of time to talk on the way to Grandma's; her house was in the foothills east of town. As it turned out, we had a lot to talk about. "I'm moving out here," he said once we were underway. "Mama fell last month."

Oh shit, I thought. Grandma was eighty-two. "She called you?"

"Yeah. She didn't ask me to move here but when I suggested it she didn't say no. So the place looks a little torn up, and she's a little freaked out, and that's why."

"Was she hurt? When she fell?"

"No, just scared." He sighed. I glanced over at him. This was the kind of thing you always know, in the back of your mind, is probably in the future. The kind of thing you hope will somehow magically not happen, so everyone will be okay forever, so nothing will change.

I thought for a while. Dad was in the Army for thirty years, till he was forty-eight. Since he went civilian, he'd been working as an orderly at the Mayo Clinic in Phoenix. Sixteen years now, and he used to say he was shooting for twenty. But plans change. Grandma most definitely did not want to move to Phoenix. Besides, Dad lived in a second-floor walk-up one-bedroom apartment there. Grandma's two-bedroom, one-and-a-half-bath house was all one level. Her friends were here, her church, her whole life. "You'll make new friends here," I said.

"Oh sure. Mama told me it's time to pick up my guitar again. I said what, find some other old guys and start a band? She said why not."

I glanced over again; he was smiling now. "You know what, you totally should. I think that would be great. Are you still coming to the wedding?" I knew Grandma wasn't. She did not fly, and it was too much of a drive for either of them given Lou and I were working the night before and planning to bug out the second we said 'I do.' We were not, in short, having an Event.

"Yeah, I'll come. She says I can put the whole thing on FaceTime for her." We laughed about that for longer than it probably deserved. Possibly because laughing over my iPhone-addicted grandma was so much easier than thinking about how this was the beginning of the end.

Once we got there, of course, we had tons to think about (and talk about). Grandma said this was the perfect time to sort through all her old stuff. She'd been living alone for the eight years since Grandpa died. Most of his stuff was still in the house. A lot of old junk of Dad's was in there too. There was even some old junk of mine. Dad had made a start on it but between us we went through closets and cupboards and drawers like a pair of Tasmanian devils.

Over dinner, he told me to tell Lou how great the little water feature was. Grandma showed me phone pictures she'd taken of all the birds, all the usual rodents, a fox, a coyote, even a bobcat. (Plus deer, of course. Put anything edible or drinkable in your yard and you will have deer.) Then she told me how she fell, and the end of that conversation was agreeing to get rid of the area rugs over slippery ceramic tile in her bedroom and the living room, and put in wall-to-wall carpet instead in both those rooms and in the hall between. I told her Lou and I would be happy to put them both up in a hotel and get some workers in so it could get done fast. Later, when she was in bed and I was having a beer with Dad, he said, "I could do that." Which was true. He didn't have Lou's design chops but he was handy enough.

I kind of glared at him and said, "Yes but you don't have to. She wants to stay here, you're giving up your bachelor pad, let us take some of the load."

He didn't say anything for a minute, only nodded and drank some beer. We were quiet for a while. I thought we were done talking for the night. Before we went to bed (me in the second bedroom and him on the couch) he said, "You know, Gloria, I'm really proud of you. I don't think I've ever said so, and I'm sorry. You're a good person and a great musician, and I'm glad your life is turning out so good."

I was so surprised, it took me a few seconds to regroup. Eventually I said thank you, and told him I loved him too (because that was really what he was saying), and then got out of the kitchen because we were both a little emotional and we just didn't do that. We were still awkward as fuck in the morning. Grandma was all, what is your damage, and it got seriously funny. We laughed all the way through the next phase of decluttering.

And then I came home. I had to bring a ton of stuff with me that Grandma didn't want to throw out. She probably knew I would throw it out, but I guess it was easier to contemplate at a remove.

Gonzo and Salma didn't get married in a casino chapel. They got married at her church. There were a lot more people there than I'd expected, which was dumb of me because her kids had friends and teachers, and there were all the people from the restaurant (which was closed for the day) with their families, and she had family. Gonzo had a ton of people too, friends he'd made on all the jobs he'd had over the years, and his family, plus Lou and me and the Rogues.

This was the first wedding I'd been to in a whole lot of years. Lou said the same thing. It was seriously lovely to see those two finally standing up together in front of the priest, with all their friends and family. We'd given Salma a little bit of crap over making Gonzo wait so long, but the truth is we understood why. And the steadfastness of their bond, the years of 'we will get through this together,' was something I hadn't seen before, not in an unmarried couple. I really hadn't seen it at all, not up close and personal.

Lou told me that was one of the things that tipped him toward asking Gonzo to be his home-building buddy. He saw in those two the same kind of commitment he saw in his parents, and he thought, if anyone can help me turn this pile of lumber into a home it is this guy.

So as you can imagine there was crying. At the ceremony, at the reception, and when we finally left to go home. Before Lou started the car I said, "You know I'm not much of one for saying sentimental things. But for the record, the fact that Ignacio González is your best friend is like a neon sign saying This Guy Values Love, and I love you."

He kissed me, and I cried a little more (he might have too). Then he said, "I love you," and we went home.

XIII – Lou

August 2016

The news from New Mexico was not so great. That Tommy was going to live with Ynez was good; she had a nice little house, and he was in good health. Plus he had all that experience from working at Mayo. Even an orderly learns how to spot trouble with a patient. With any luck, having company would give her a new lease on life. And this was happening before a serious illness or injury. Being so healthy at eighty-two was good. I planned to suggest making a Christmas visit a regular thing.

Plus, from the sound of things, it was way past time for those closets to get cleared out. Gloria's series of texts about that project was hilarious. She warned me that she was bringing some shit home. Specifically: *OMG Lou I'm going to look like a bag lady.*

Paloma was not any more thrilled about being left alone than I was, after those almost-two-weeks of near-constant companionship. But it was only one night. Kathy Donovan did us a favor and picked Gloria up at McCarran. I could have gotten some time off from work, but we'd actually identified a problem and I was working on the solution.

One big part of on-the-floor enforcement is simply cruising the tables to back up the dealers. If players won't keep their hands off the craps or blackjack felt, for example, or if there's a lot of fidgeting around the roulette wheel, you want to be sure somebody's not trying to distract another player, or confuse the dealer, or swipe a chip, or whatever. Sometimes it wasn't even about the game, it was a screen for a pickpocket.

Anyway, what we were looking into was something completely different.

We had a high-stakes poker room, with a regular schedule of tournaments. Some of them were streamed live, and a lot of money changed hands. I had a big file already on the regular players. These guys – mostly men – were from all over. They didn't play only in our room. Some of them played all over the world. One of our dealers had noticed a trend of longtime winners being edged out when a certain new guy was in the room.

Now, anybody can have a lucky streak, and one guy's lucky streak always means other people are losing. We hadn't seen anything yet in the fair-play footage to indicate interference on the table. This hadn't been going on so long that the lucky streak looked excessive. We were keeping an eye on it, though, and we had a few things to do. The room's manager was going to strike up some casual conversation with a few of the recent losers to see what they had to say about the games. We were flagging the new guy, and putting extra eyes on that room when he was playing. And I'd written a script for my bosses to review. Once approved, I talked to my counterparts at the other casinos who did this kind of business. We wanted to know where else this guy was playing, or if they'd noticed a different new guy who was having the same kind of lucky streak.

If there was anything malfeasant going on, obviously we wanted to stop it fast. I had an idea about it that was kind of out there. So out there, I hadn't even brought it up yet. It was based on nothing more than experience, a few too many years noticing something wrong, combined with what seemed, on the surface, to be clean play.

Gloria was back at work, the things she liberated from New Mexico either safely disposed around the house or silently released into the wild via Goodwill. After Gonzo and Salma's wedding she had said a few frustrated words and gone back into the music room. I still wasn't sure exactly what she was doing, but I knew she wanted it a certain way before she let Gino hear it. Her being a little preoccupied was a good thing. Two of my teammates and I brought in reports that, taken separately, looked fairly innocuous. It wasn't until they were put together with my far-out idea that we all said, hmm.

First, there was one server always present when Lucky New Guy was playing. She was present at other times, too; but it was a consistent thing. Second, Lucky New Guy was playing at two of the other casinos. They hadn't spotted the trend yet. Now they were ramping up all the same observation and analysis we were doing. Third, our regulars noted an increase in errors-in-play. Ill-judged bets, missed opportunities. Bear in mind, these are professionals. They did not play impulsively. They weren't at the table to be big shots and make a splash. They were there to make money. So when more than a few of them said things like 'I lost focus' or 'I read the cards wrong' or even 'I missed that bluff' I put two and two together and got five.

It was still an out-there idea, so I asked to talk to the enforcement managers privately. I told them what I thought was happening and they looked at me like I was crazy. Then somebody said, "How could we verify?"

The obvious thing was to fire that server, but if we did we'd never get proof. There was no chance she was working alone. We needed to keep her on until we verified her presence was part of the problem. We just had to make it impossible for her to do what I thought she was doing, namely introducing some kind of make-you-lose into the beverage service. There are a lot of substances that can cause confusion, blurred vision, loss of concentration, memory lapses. Most of them aren't even illegal. It's only when you dose someone without their knowledge and consent that a crime is committed. Nobody else thought of this because nobody else had ever investigated date rape.

Lucky New Guy was definitely a bastard if he was having this woman do his dirty work. We'd have to get her to roll on him. Usually a casino likes to deal with cheaters quietly, but this was actual assault (if I was right). Unfortunately, banning the guy might be the best we could do. Because now that this was in our minds, we couldn't let it happen again.

The next time we spotted Lucky New Guy, the new beverage plan went into action. All drinks were free in the high-stakes room. A lot of the players didn't drink alcohol when they were in a game, but nearly all drank something. We had a cover story ready to deploy, and some extra people on duty. It wasn't as non-obvious as it would have been in a movie. The reason it worked was it played like a special treat. That suspect server was discreetly removed from the room. Lucky New Guy had to pretend he didn't notice. All the drinks were delivered by the new people, who all happened to be moonlighting showgirls.

There were miles of fishnet-covered legs in the room. One of our people had a quiet word with the one female player to advise her we were running an internal security operation, the servers would be slightly egregious, but this was not a sign that the room was for men only. She almost cracked us up later by giving the camera this 'really?!' stare on her way out.

Anyway, Lucky New Guy actually was a legit player, so he didn't lose big or fast. He also didn't win. Everybody else was sharp, and at the change of shift the results were back to normal. Our people had a cop on hand with a warrant to search the server. When Not-So-Lucky New Guy eventually busted out, we caught up with him too.

The server was not an idiot. She instantly gave him up. She told us all about the drug they'd been using. She told us who her counterparts were at the other two casinos. They wouldn't be caught in the act, but their testimony would weigh on him. One of our security guys was stationed in the room with the cheater, listening through an earpiece, not talking to the guy at all. I'm told the guy started looking really nervous after a half hour or so, and some other way when the cop came in to read him his rights.

So then we had to decide whether we were going to tell the other players that they'd been played. We couldn't prove that anyone had been given anything. We had a conspiracy on our hands for sure, but the D.A. couldn't give us good odds on successful prosecution. The casinos hadn't lost money. Some of the players had. There was no chance that they could get any of it back through the courts. Gambling was an 'at your own risk' proposition any way you looked at it.

All the same: these were our customers. They'd been rooked on our turf. So ultimately what we decided to do was set up a closed tournament. We came up with some way to link all these players and plausibly account for them being invited. We gave them a reasonable three-figure buy-in, put up a six-figure tourney prize, and put some money in the pot for every hand. If anyone went bust, we were prepared to stake him again, but nobody did. Everybody was getting their share of the luck. At the end of the game, everybody was in a very good mood.

This was not such a far-out thing to do. You want your tourney players and your high rollers to keep coming back. It cost us, sure. But now, instead of deciding to play somewhere else, those guys would all come back. When they noticed that they never saw Lucky New Guy again they might figure something out. They might figure we'd caught him doing something and couldn't prove it, couldn't quantify their losses, so we set up the tourney as an apology, plus an assurance that they would continue to get the fairest possible play at our house. Which was of course exactly what we did.

This kind of cheating was something you heard about in sports, like in the bad old days of horse racing when a groom might be bribed to give a horse too much water or the wrong kind of food before a race, to slow it down. Our cheater had played well. Not well enough to take on that level of opponents, as we saw when they weren't impaired. He probably had an interesting story to tell about how he had the idea and how he got people to work with him. I don't know what he told the cops. I'd have to follow up with one of my buddies to find out what they eventually charged him with. Or if they couldn't come up with anything, and had to let him go.

We did our part, anyway. We got the word out in the gaming community. Before long, servers in those high-stakes rooms everywhere were being issued new uniforms with no pockets.

This took a couple of months to play out. Gloria knew we had a situation, but I couldn't really tell her about it until it was all over. When I gave her the short version, she said, "Way to show up, new guy," which made me laugh.

Then she asked if we considered sitting me down in the tourney and I said, "Oh no. Cheating to lose, if the real players ever found out, they'd never forgive us. Besides, none of them knew me. If I sat down in there, they'd be like, who the fuck are you."

"Are you that anonymous?"

"People recognize me out on the main floor. But it's better for everybody if people like me are invisible where the real money's moving. We don't want to be obvious." This conversation was happening on the couch at home, late at night. Paloma was curled up in one of her cushy beds, I had my arm around Gloria, and it seemed like it might be time to move on to the bedroom. Especially when she turned her head and kissed me. Even more especially when she turned her whole body toward mine and put her hand on my chest, then under the waistband of my shorts.

"Speaking of obvious," she said against my neck. She did a few things with her hand. "It is obvious that this should be in my mouth."

"Jesus, Gloria." I dug my hand into her hair and closed my eyes.

XIII – Gloria

August 2016

First let me say I was still pretty happy with my rough demo for 'Thief of Hearts.' But after the wedding I had to go in and make it sweeter. I realized I'd let the conflict-driven energy of 'Hit Me' carry over. Energy had to be there, but what I needed now was that sense of mutually-supportive let's-do-this commitment that Gonzo and Salma had. Maybe I shied away from it because that was also me and Lou, and it felt too personal. I'd never written anything personal before, not for publication. (Everybody who writes anything probably has a private stash of what amounts to diary entries. Some artists publish all that. Not me.)

So while Lou was dealing with a situation at work, I was back to my usual schedule. Nine shows a week, plus a few hours of arrangement and rehearsal. Gino brought in a list of things he wanted to add to his sets here and there. With a catalog as huge as Frank Sinatra's there was a lot of scope for variation. The rest of my available time went to fixing the new songs. Like I said, they didn't have to be perfect. I was spoiled, that was all. I was used to handing something to Gino and getting no critique. Sometimes it seemed like we were using the same brain.

I knew this revision was the right thing to do because he was not cagey about being in love. He sang 'What If It Were True' regularly, and he always dedicated it to Sergei. He mentioned 'my husband' on stage nearly every night. He was not a cynic, and while he could play a cynic perfectly well – he could play bitter, angry, vengeful; the man had chops – I wanted his own true sweet character to come through on the album. He and Gonzo had a lot in common under the skin.

I really dithered about playing the stuff for Lou before Gino. I hadn't done that with 'Hit Me' because we were brand-new then. But we were almost a year in; we were engaged; it felt like he should be the first to hear the songs. So the Monday after his big situation got resolved, I sat him down in the living room, slid the disc into the stereo, and fled the scene. When the music stopped I was in the spare room with Paloma, flat on my back on the bed, staring at the ceiling. "Doing it a shade darker than the walls was a good choice," I said when I heard Lou come in.

"Well, this room gets more light than yours," he said. "Those are great songs, honey."

I sat up. "I didn't even put in the lyrics." I could make a noise that was technically singing; I could carry a tune; but my voice was like a combination of Amy Winehouse and Tom Waits. Thus, I did not record it. "The melodies were clear enough?"

"The melodies were terrific. I can't wait to hear them when they're finished." He sat beside me. I leaned my shoulder against his. He turned his head to kiss my cheek. "Does Gonzo know you were doing this?"

"Sort of. I don't know if he understood the scope of the project. I'm positive he didn't understand he'll get a royalty. I mean, it's going to be tiny, but the thing was his idea. I couldn't not give him a credit."

"You could put a picture of him and Salma in the liner notes."

"We totally should! Oh my God. We should use pictures of him for every song. Sepia-tone, like old-timey pictures. People will be like, is that Pedro Pascal?

Is that Burt Reynolds?" Lou was snickering. "The way things have been going lately, he'll probably end up with a career as a model. That's got to be one of the top ten mustaches in the world." Lou laughed out loud. I went for the big question. "So you think it's ready to hand to Gino?"

"Absolutely. You think the trumpet guy is going to like this color?" He was looking around the room. We'd painted it after Gonzo left, the same silvery blue as my music room. The darker ceiling made it feel nicely moody. "What do you hear from him lately?"

I answered the second question first. "There's progress. If he decides to crash out here he'll probably like the color fine. It looks like something he would wear." Lou snorted. That was one of the many things I loved about him: my nonsense always made him laugh. "Thank you for liking my shit."

"Your music is not shit. Want to drop it off at Gino's before we go to La Cholla?"

"Sure. Good idea. I know he knows I've been cooking something up."

"He knows you." Lou's tone was the tiniest bit dry. "Let's take an inventory before we go in. I keep forgetting what kind of food we have on hand."

"God, me too. Maybe if Scott moves in he'll be good about stocking the fridge." I patted Lou's thigh and stood up. Not without regret, because we were wearing next to nothing. "Let me go print the lyric sheets." While I was doing that I sent a text to Gino: *Hey boss have something for you to listen to. OK to drop off in about an hour?*

He was probably lounging around the pool with his husband; Mondays were a day off for Sergei too. A

187

reply came back fast: *Sure thing. We'll put some pants on*

I laughed to myself. I'd never seen him naked but he made enough comments like that for me to guess that when other people weren't around, he and Sergei were nudists like me and Lou. *Not on my account. I'll leave it in the music room, you'll never even know I was there. See you tomorrow*

Great I'll cancel the pants. See you tomorrow. How could you not love a boss like that? I put the package together and went to get dressed.

So Lou drove us into town; I sneaked into Gino and Sergei's house and left the album package in the music room; we went to dinner; we got a carload of groceries. We went home, unloaded, took Paloma for a walk and then stripped off again and fooled around. A great day, one of a series of great days in this new, wonderful, coupled life.

The next few weeks were business as usual except, first, we found out that 'Behind the Strip' was going to go for another thirteen episodes; and second, I was meeting up with Gino and the Rogues to work on 'Thief of Hearts.' There was a solid chance, let's call it a near-certainty, that I would never delete the email Gino sent me after listening to the demo. Suffice to say it made me feel really good about my music, and about working with him for the rest of my life, or his life. Preferably my life. It was so nice that I forwarded it to Grandma. She told me she showed it to Dad. Then he sent me a text saying *Don't suppose you need a guitar player*. He put a smiley face on it as if to say it was a joke, and at first I dismissed it. Then I thought, hmm. It was highly likely that Spanish guitar would be used on at least some of the tracks. The only problem was, I hadn't heard him play for years. I wasn't sure how to approach it, so I asked Lou. He was good at the family stuff.

Like he always did, Lou considered the question before saying, "Have you and the guys talked about other instruments yet?"

"Only the off-chance that Scott will be around." That was yet-undetermined. I knew he was still interested in collaborating with Ruben and Oscar. "I mean, even if he decides not to move out here he'll probably play on the thing. But no, we're going to finish the four-part arrangements before we start adding anything."

"You used electric guitars on 'Hit Me.'"

"Mmm. This might be all acoustic. I really need to hear him," I admitted, with a distinct sense of 'eek.' Because what if I brought it up as a possibility, but then he couldn't cut it? I had literally no idea what he could do, or how he was to work with. Add the complication of me being the daughter whose music career he'd always seemed to resent, and it felt like disaster waiting to happen. I knew I didn't need to say all that, but I did anyway. Then I said, "But when I went out to see them last month things were different. Maybe this is my chance to really fix things. If he's up to it."

Lou put his hand on the back of my neck, under my hair, and squeezed a little. "It's not your job to fix it." I made a semi-dissenting sound. He shook me gently. "You could have him work with Ruben and Oscar. They'd know. They could be the ones to say yes or no."

"Yes! You're a genius. Exactamundo." I leaned over and kissed him. We were in bed, so that went a predictable direction. Calling him a genius met with approval from several quarters, apparently. Or like all

189

four quarters. God, he was sexy. We didn't talk about music any more that night.

A couple days later I heard from Scott, and he was definitely coming out to Las Vegas for a while, so we made some plans. I told Ruben and Oscar and they got totally excited. When I mentioned the Dad guitar question, they were so thrilled about Scott they didn't even flinch. Oscar said, "Yeah, send him a copy of your demo and tell him to contact me when he has something ready."

"You don't mind? Because he might suck." I felt like I had to say that.

"He might," Ruben said. "Then again he might not. You had to get it from somewhere." That was both true and flattering, so I sent off the demo to Dad with a set of the lyric sheets, Oscar's contact information, and a note saying 'I hope it works out!' Which was sincere. It was also totally passing the buck, but I suspected that would be a relief for Dad. After all, he had no idea this was even coming his way. How much freakier would it be to think he had to get *my* approval? Even though he did.

Anyway, I got that out of the way and abruptly realized it was two weeks till the wedding. My dress had not arrived. I pinged my dressmaker: *So how's it going?* With a smiley face.

Lourdes wrote back immediately: *I will bring it to the casino tonight!!* Which got me all excited. Except I had to settle down and get ready because we needed some extra time to rehearse before the show. We were working on a couple of numbers, Sinatra classics we'd been doing all along, but with a Latin twist. Gino had suggested it after we started on the new songs. We were planning to put these fresh arrangements in the set about a week from now, which coincidentally was the date I was expecting Scott Easton to show up. I'd sort of invited Kathy Donovan too. I knew she thought he was the hotness, and after the summer he'd had I figured he might be up for a diversion.

I wouldn't say I was matchmaking but, well, maybe I was. Kathy was a few years older than me and single. Scott was my age and single. She loved music; he was a musician. They were both good-looking and straight, self-employed, in the entertainment industry, and why not. A bad date was the worst that could happen, and she had thirteen more episodes of TV to write. A bad date would be great material.

Plus, scheming about Kathy and Scott would keep my mind off the fact that in very few days I would be marrying Lou. I was way too excited about it. Our life was not going to change in any significant way, so why be so excited? Impossible question. Seeing the dress that night didn't help. It was exactly what I hoped for. I tried it on; it fit perfectly; I squealed to myself and put my regular dress back on. Then sent a text to Lourdes: *I.O.U.*

XIV – Lou

September 2016

The trumpet player finally rolled into town eight days before our wedding. Gloria texted me as soon as she knew he was there. He was going to stay at her casino for a few nights, and come to the show that night. I knew Gino and the gang were planning to do a couple Latin-style arrangements of classic Sinatra numbers as kind of a teaser for the new record. Gloria was going to have dinner with the guy after the show. I might have minded except she also told me she was trying to throw him and Kathy together. So I went on home after my shift, took Paloma for a little moonlit walk, fixed myself something to eat, and waited to hear how it went.

"Honey?" She called out before she even closed the front door.

"In the living room."

"We *killed* tonight. Oh my God Lou." She came around the fireplace, checked for small-dog hazards, and flung herself onto the couch beside me. I wrapped an arm around her and pulled her over for a kiss. "Mmm. You're sexy. You taste like, what is that."

"Flan."

"Oh no you didn't. Is there some for me?"

"Do I want to live?"

She laughed, kissed me again, and wriggled into cuddle position. "'My Way' in Spanish. Fucking *ace*. I was too busy to look at the audience but Scott told me he could feel it in the room when they caught on. It was huge. Gino's never sounded better. Kathy said when she heard that she was like, fuck, what is he going to close with, because people were going nuts. Then we did 'Boulevard of Broken Dreams,' it was that quiet rumba arrangement, and I've heard it a dozen times now but it still gets me. Kathy said Scott was practically crying at the table."

"So you went to dinner," I prompted.

"Which, I don't know why I bothered, because if those two aren't in bed right now they're kidding themselves. Could have just pointed them at each other and said go for it!" I snickered. She rested her head on my shoulder. "I mean okay, it was fun. We talked music, we talked nonsense. They both went to the john and I texted Kathy saying go for it. As soon as Scott got back I said hey gotta go see you tomorrow and made tracks." She was grinning. "He's coming out here tomorrow afternoon. This afternoon."

I squeezed her a little. "So you think he's going to stay?" She nodded. "What else."

"Well, we were bullshitting about what he could play at our wedding and Kathy goes, how about the paso doble. So he may be playing that."

"Uh," I started, because I had no idea what that was.

"Trust me." She turned her head and kissed me again. "It's going to kick ass."

And because Gloria was as much of a goofball as me about some things but she was not a goofball about music, I trusted her. If she said it would kick ass, that's all I needed to know. I nuzzled her neck. "I could help you get out of this dress."

"Yes, you could." She got off the couch, gave me a hand up, and sashayed ahead of me to the master. Those dresses really made for some impressive sashay. As did the high-heeled saddle shoes, and the hips. The second she stopped walking I had my hands on her waist, stroking up to cup her breasts. "Mmm, Lou."

"You're so beautiful." She made another yummy sound while I unzipped the dress, stood still while I lifted it over her head, then helpfully wriggled as I tugged the crinoline down over her bottom. She put a hand on my head for balance as she stepped out of it. The floof of tulle landed on top of her dress, on the purple leather armchair we'd recently added to the room. It was pure luck because I wasn't really watching to see where it landed. I was on my knees with my mouth on Gloria's ass while I peeled off her underwear. One hand stroking up one of those curvy legs, the other one holding her still against my mouth. I heard something else land on the chair and glanced over; it was her bra. "Turn around."

"Are you going to eat me out right here?" She turned around.

"Mm-hmm," I said. She had both hands on my head, riding my face, already starting to make some of those porny sounds that drove me crazy. I wished I could see this. My gorgeous Glory, naked except for her shoes, and me with my face buried in her pussy. On my knees, right where she'd had me from the start. She tasted so good. I had two fingers up inside her. I felt her grip them and knew she was getting close. Jesus, what that woman could do to me. I was desperate to put a hand on myself but, due to poor impulse control, my jeans were still securely fastened. Should have gotten naked before she got home. *Next time*, I thought hazily, right before she bucked against me.

"God damn!"

"Mmm." I licked her again, felt the pulse. Quick and shallow. She might go again if I played my cards right. I stood up slowly, dragging my lips and tongue up her body to her breasts, her throat, her mouth.

She pressed against me, strong and warm. "I'll bet you want those jeans off." She unbuttoned, unzipped. Helped me push them down. I pulled my tee shirt over my head, then stepped out of the jeans. "Why did you even put those on when you got home?"

"Stupid." She laughed. I followed her over to the bed, where she pulled down the covers, then sat down and lifted a foot. I unbuckled the shoe, waited for the other one. Took them over to the chair and put them on the floor. No, I don't throw shoes. For one thing, there's a dopey little dog in the house. The dog in question was currently watching the humans do human sex things from her bed under the window. I was back at our bed, standing between Gloria's legs. She had her mouth on my body, and my cock in her hand. Both my hands were on her shoulders, beside her neck. I wanted to watch her stroke me, so I tipped her chin up. "Let me see."

"What, this?" She made a production out of it. "Want to see me do this too?" She licked me. I made some kind of sound. I wanted to be inside her. We hadn't done that for a while. "You know," she said, with her mouth touching me, "I love stroking you off. And I love sucking you off. But I'd really love it if you'd fuck me right now." My cock jumped against her lips and she took it again, hard and tight, then let me go and scooted backward. I followed her fast, bending down for a kiss, letting her hook her hand around the back of my neck and pull me to her. I settled between her legs, propped on my elbows, kissing her while I slid against her. So hot, so wet, making noises as hungry as mine. I raised up a little, positioned myself. Then it was the unbelievable sweet torture of waiting for her to take me. Rocking her hips, letting an inch sink in. Then another. Hands on my hips to tell me when. This, exactly this, was why I did so many damned push-ups and planks. Halfway there. Eyes closed, completely focused on how she felt around me. There would be a moment, after I was all the way in, when the adjustment was complete and everything relaxed. Only then could I move. When she was this ready we didn't need lube to get there. "Mmm. Baby." Her voice was low and throaty, and her hand was on my ass. I put my mouth on hers and pulled halfway out. Slowly in again, listening to her breath, feeling her rise to meet me.

This was the best, the absolute best. Knowing how to get there, knowing she wanted me, all of me. I could do anything right now and she wouldn't mind. Those minutes of control set me up for more of it. Slow, deep, hearing her breath hitch as she ground against me. A foot hooked over my thigh. That strong hand pulling me in. Then her pace quickening. Breath vocal, like mine. Not kissing anymore because we needed air, but faces close together. I felt her tighten around me as the pitch of her sounds rose. Had to keep doing exactly what I was doing, had to get her there, *God, please, Gloria, now oh fuck oh Christ yes NOW.*

"Holy ungh!" Then she was gripping me, pulsing around me, and I held completely still until those contractions eased. She slapped my ass and I took off like a racehorse. "Go, goddammit, go Lou *yes* baby oh my *fuck* you're such a *YES!!*"

I was throbbing, sunk deep in her, too much of my weight on her, gasping. Pushed up, went for another kiss. "Mmm. I love you."

"I love you too. Get off me."

Impossible not to laugh. I pulled out slowly, because it still felt awfully good in there. All the way

196

back till I was sitting on my heels, letting my spine settle down. A few minor contortions to be done, ending with rolling my neck. I was so well-rested and non-stressed-out these days, I didn't need to do the same kind of flexibility work that Officer Kravitz required.

There was a nightlight in the bathroom that gave enough light for us to see each other. Gloria was watching me. "You are amazingly right for me," she said. "Perfect, in fact."

"Same goes."

"I'd better take my makeup off." She rolled over and belly-crawled to the edge of the bed, swung a leg down, and only then tried to stand up. "Whew. When Kravitz fucks you, you know you've been fucked." I snorted, laughed silently, and followed her to the bathroom.

I left for work before the trumpet guy got out to the house on Friday. I didn't see him on Saturday, either. Gloria told him to come out for brunch on Sunday and to bring Kathy. Apparently they'd spent a lot of time together since Thursday night. Like basically all of it, except for the hours he was out at our place practicing. I told Gloria I was going to make a pitch.

"About building a house?"

"Mm-hmm." We'd talked about it here and there for the best part of a year. I hadn't pursued it with Gonzo because Salma owned her house, and it had become clear that she didn't want to leave it. But Ruben and Oscar were still possibilities, and if Scott and Kathy were falling in love then he was also a possibility. And he had money now. If the idea took him the way it took me, and if we got along, we might be able to work a deal. "I know he's only been here for a minute, and I haven't really even talked to the guy. But you like him. Gino and Sergei like him. Ruben and Oscar like him, and now Kathy likes him. If he likes the music village idea, do you think he'd put in some money?"

Gloria had obviously been thinking about this too. "He might bankroll the whole thing. He sold his mother's house in Pacific Palisades, and I looked it up online. It went for seven million."

"Damn!"

"Yeah, that's what I said. I know you've run the numbers."

That I had. My specs for three new houses were essentially at the point where all I needed was a good excuse to take them in to the permitting office. And money. And a reasonable way to account for the value of my land, the liquid capital, and rental or purchase agreements. If Easton decided to go in with me, we'd have to talk to a lawyer or two. I dragged my mind back to the current conversation. "Each one would cost more than this one, because we need access and utilities first. But all three should come in under seven hundred and fifty." She knew that meant 'thousand.'

"Well, shit, Lou. Unless you guys hate each other, it sounds like a good investment. For everybody. Plus oh my God if the four of us were out here we could make so much noise."

She sounded so excited. I was cracking up. "Let's get some sleep, baby. Tomorrow might be a big day."

XIV – Gloria

September 2016

From my point of view, the biggest takeaway from our brunch with Scott and Kathy was that he and Lou were going into the house-building business together. Also that, while Scott liked the proposed floor plan (exactly like our house), he wanted his guest room to be a recording studio. He also wanted a lap pool. Naturally these stipulations met with my complete approval. I had a chance to talk to him some more about it the next day, when he went with me and Ruben and Oscar to meet with the Carbon 13 people about scoring the next set of episodes for 'Behind the Strip.' That was also when he told them about the music village idea. This added a lot of excitement in a week that was already kind of packed.

The parents were coming in Thursday night. All four of them said they'd be coming to Gino's show. We would then have dinner together, with Lou. My mother was advised that everyone was there to have a good time and be happy, and that if she couldn't say something nice, to do something else with her mouth. My father was completely chill.

When the demo and lyric sheets landed he sent me a text that amounted to 'what the fuck.' I got a more coherent one a couple of days later, and one from Grandma the day after that saying *Tu padre está loco.* When I stopped giggling and asked for details, she wrote *He loves this music, he never stops playing it. He is talking to that bass player of yours. Very happy!*

I wrote *Glad to hear it. Maybe he can jam with the guys after the wedding. Are you well? Is it okay having him there?*

Chica it's good. Especially because he's happy. Tu hiciste eso, gracias. The new rug is so nice underfoot. Send me that wedding on FaceTime

LOL you got it. Te amo abuelita

Te amo también

We didn't have anything out of the ordinary planned for the Thursday-night show. People were kind of starting to expect that, I think, but if we went too far off-book on a regular basis the book would stop being the book. And the show was 'Gino Corsetti and The Desert Rogues,' but it was also a Sinatra tribute show. So most of the time, we kept it canon. Which was fine, because we all had a lot of other stuff going on and why complicate things for ourselves.

Dinner with the parents was fine. Even my mother was well-behaved. Lou's parents were perfect, as usual. They asked what kind of music we were going to have at the wedding. I said, "Gino is going to sing something, and my friend Scott is going to play something."

Elizabeth was thrilled about Gino, of course. She and Samuel were huge fans. "That young man we met at your show tonight?" she said. "What does he play?"

"He's a trumpet expert," I said. "A bunch of other horns, too, but tomorrow it'll be the trumpet. Kathy, the woman you saw him with, the writer? She suggested this thing, and I liked it, and he was all challenge accepted, so long story short it's a very nontraditional version of the wedding march." Samuel was cracking up.

"Well, what's it called?" Elizabeth had this face that said she completely expected to know whatever it was he would be playing.

"It's called 'España Cani,'" I said. "Better known as the paso doble."

"The *what*?"

I was grinning at her, my dad was laughing, Lou was laughing. "You know, like, show me your paso doble." She looked blank. I was appalled. "You haven't seen 'Strictly Ballroom?' Elizabeth, I'm about to be your daughter-in-law. I would not steer you wrong. Watch that movie. That's not the paso doble in the movie but who cares." I pulled my phone out of my pocket and texted the title to her so she wouldn't forget. "By the way have I thanked you lately? You and Samuel?"

"For what?"

"For making Lou. He is awesome." I glanced over. He was giving me this soft look. I blew him a kiss, then turned back to Elizabeth. "Tell Leah we'll have a party with them next time we're in Jersey. Things are so crazy right now we couldn't make this easier for anyone but us." Lou's sister had sent back an email saying, basically, 'you had to do this on a Friday?' and promising they would see us soon. She had three kids, they were in school, we were jerks.

Elizabeth patted my hand. "I completely understand. You know when Samuel and I got married it was at the justice of the peace."

"Jewish man and Italian woman," Samuel said. "It would have been five hundred people and it would have taken three days." Even my mother laughed.

"We got married at the courthouse too," my dad said unexpectedly. "We couldn't afford a big thing."

Samuel shook his head. "Nobody can. What these kids are doing is smart. Spend the money on the house."

"And on a dirty weekend in Cabo," I said with satisfaction. Mom rolled her eyes. Dad made a 'too much information' face, which was ridiculous given

201

Lou and I had been living together for eight months. So, since while I was totally psyched and excited to be getting married I was also a little nervous, I threw Dad under the bus and said, "Did you work up something for Ruben and Oscar?"

And what do you know. He grabbed the conversational ball and took off running. He told everybody all about the demo I sent, and the lyrics, and the back story, and how he used to play guitar a lot. How he was getting back to it now that he was retired. How they were going to jam for a while tomorrow, after Lou and I left for Cabo. "It's really been fun," he said. "Even if they decide I shouldn't play on the record, it's been great. Me and some buddies of mine in Santa Fe are going to see about playing at this restaurant near my mother's house. They do live music there."

Mom's face was such a Who Are You face. They didn't talk, so I figured all this would be a complete surprise. I really hoped she wouldn't say something nasty. I just about fell off my chair when she said, "I'm glad you're getting back to your music, Tommy. It was good for you."

"Thanks. I appreciate that." They exchanged these cautious smiles, and I knew they were never going to be more than friendly (if they ever had been) but it was nice to think maybe they wouldn't be at each other's throats all the time anymore.

Thinking it might be a good idea to end the evening on that high note, I said, "Well this has been fun but we have to go home. I'm told there is a thing we have to get to tomorrow, at about the time we're usually getting out of bed. Thank you all for coming."

There was a chorus of good-nights and drive-carefullys and sleep-wells, a round of hugs, and a few suggestions (from me) about the best things to order from the breakfast room-service menu. Then Lou and I got out of there. We drove in separately, of course, so he walked me to my car and gave me a kiss. "See you at home, Ms. Bartolo," he said.

"Do you wish I was changing my name?"

He made this 'are you kidding' face. "I seriously considered changing *mine*." I laughed, kissed him again, and got in the car. "Drive safe, baby."

"You too. I love you."

"I love you."

I checked my rear-view mirror as I rolled out of the parking lot. He was still standing there, the way he had been that time after our first walk. My God, what a year it had been. I was very attentive to traffic on the way home. This was not the time to have a fender-bender. When I got to the house, I took Paloma for a short walk even though Scott's car was there and he'd probably taken her out. "You like your babysitter all right, don't you, cutie?" She was nosing around one of the clumps of grass in the yard. "He'll look after you till we get back on Monday. Of course, Kathy will probably be here a lot so he might be a little distracted, but you're used to that. Ready to go in? Good girl. Wipe your feet. There ya go." We went inside, I gave her a bedtime snack, and then I went to get undressed. Lou would be there any minute and I thought it might be a good idea to already be in bed acting sleepy. We had the whole weekend to fool around. I didn't want to be late to my own wedding. It seemed like forever till he finally got there. "Where the hell have you been?"

I could hear him laughing under his breath. "I took a walk before I started back. Figured it would be good to wind down a little."

"Yeah, you need a full night's sleep." He bent over and kissed me, then went to the bathroom to wash up. Now that he was home, I could relax for real. When he slid into bed beside me I pressed close, put my head on his shoulder, and felt him wrap an arm over me. "Good night, Lou."

"Good night, Gloria." He kissed my forehead. I think I went to sleep almost immediately.

In the morning I was as hyped as if I was going to play at the Grammys. Lou was a little jazzed too. We did not fool around, even in the shower. We didn't waste time. He was out of there before me because I had some extra grooming to do. While I was doing my hair and makeup, I heard him out in the kitchen with Scott, laughing about something or other. "You could at least bring me a cup of coffee," I yelled, and a minute later Scott did. "You're lucky I have my robe on."

"I was hoping you wouldn't. All these years and I've never seen you naked."

"Smart-ass. When you get your pool I'll go skinny-dipping in it." He laughed and left me alone. I tasted the coffee; it was just right. Lou must have fixed it. Now I had a few minutes to stretch before I put my dress on. I got down on the floor with the mug, imagining the beach at Cabo. I'd only been there once before, a long time ago. A whole weekend with Lou, and nobody else, and nothing to do. It was going to be great. When I finished my coffee I bounced up and went into Final Bridal Preparation.

God, I loved this dress. It was exactly the same pattern Lourdes always used, but in this perfect iridescent grey silk. She did a fancy border on it for me, a wide strip of white crocheted lace, embellished with iridescent grey rhinestones. I didn't bother zipping it up yet because Lou liked doing that. I did fasten the hook at the top because I didn't want him getting a sneak peek at my fancy (and very expensive) new bra. The matching knickers were well-hidden under my black crinoline. Hair pinned up; new sparkly ornament in place; matching earrings. I checked myself out in the mirror. Not for a minute did I regret getting those rose tattoos around my neck. I loved the way they looked.

I will confess to having browsed a few wedding magazines, even though we were doing this the quick and easy way, with basically no planning required from me. One thing I kept seeing was how this was the bride's day, and a bride wanted to look her absolute best. Well, I thought it should be *our* day, but I honestly think I did look as good as I ever had or ever would. And I could not wait to marry Lou.

I heard him walk in. "Hey Glory, how are you – holy cats. That is *amazing*. You look incredible." He stepped up behind me and did the zipper. Looked over my shoulder into the mirror. "It's a good thing a bunch of people will be taking pictures."

I smiled at him. "You look pretty good too, Mr. Kravitz. Ready to go get married?"

"Am I ever." He pressed a kiss to the side of my face.

XV – Lou

September 2016

Our wedding day. Unbelievable.

Since Scott was playing for us, and since we were leaving immediately after the ceremony, he was going to drive us into town. Gloria and I were both a little keyed up. Neither of us wanted breakfast, and maybe we didn't really need coffee. But once I was done with the whole grooming thing (mine didn't take long), and dressed except for my suit jacket, I left her alone to do her thing and went out to the kitchen.

Scott was there, fully dressed. He'd taken Paloma for a walk and had coffee already made. He said, "You'd better eat something. This is almost guaranteed to be the biggest performance of your life," which made me laugh. So I scavenged something. When we heard Gloria yelling about coffee, I fixed her a mug and let Scott take it through to her. It's funny how much a part of the household he'd become in a week. We chatted for a while after he joined me again, keeping an eye on the clock. When it got to be about that time I went to the master to see if Gloria needed anything.

Does every man see the woman he loves on their wedding day and want to fall on his knees with gratitude? I hope so. I managed not to actually do that. I zipped up her dress, said something about how amazing she looked, and then got out of there with our already-packed weekend bags while she muttered something about shoes.

I've mentioned she wears those vintage-looking high-heeled saddle shoes on stage. Her whole look for this wedding was like her stage look, but turned up to eleven. The hair a bit more polished, ornamented with something sparkly. Long sparkly earrings, and some kind of sparkly makeup accenting the roses tattooed around her neck. The silky dress in a gray much too pearly to be drab. Lace, and more sparkles, and that fluffy black crinoline underneath. Her shoes were new ones, in gray and a purple so dark it was almost black. The heels were completely covered with the same gray rhinestones that were on the dress. Complete movie-star glamour. I made a mental note to suggest she should wear this outfit the next time she went to the Grammys. Scott was ready with his phone when she walked out. She posed for several pictures, for once not acting like she wanted to run away from the camera. Then she said, "Enough of that shit, let's get this show on the road."

We both said "See you soon" to Paloma. Scott took Gloria's bag, I took mine, we all got in the car.

Scott started the engine, but before putting it in gear said, "Wallets, passports, and marriage license?" We checked our pockets. All the essentials were accounted for. We also had more than one bandanna apiece. He nodded, checked the mirrors (there was never anything in the road, but he'd been driving in L.A. forever; it was habit), and backed out.

Gloria was pretty well-known in Las Vegas now, and looking the way she did today, she turned heads as we went through the casino to the chapel. We were holding hands. I will confess mine was a little warm, not to say sweaty. My thumb kept going to her engagement ring. I couldn't wait to put the wedding band beside it.

There was a room alongside the chapel for the wedding party to assemble. That was only me, Gloria, and Tommy. He was looking fine in a navy-blue suit with a bolo tie and cowboy boots. He said, "M'hija, you look beautiful." We shook hands, all trying not too obviously to watch the clock. Next door we could hear people arriving, making conversation. Sergei and Gino would be in the front row on one side with Scott. Derek, the guitar player dude from 'Behind the Strip,' was hanging out with the celebrant in what Gloria called the green room. It was probably the most accurate word for it. Derek was going to accompany Gino.

Our four parents would be seated together in the front row on the other side. Tommy was so chill I wasn't worried about him at all. That whole guitar thing, maybe combined with a complete change of environment, seemed to have let him reinvent himself a little. Dawn was on her best behavior the night before; if she could keep a lid on it today we'd be golden. How's that for a way to think about your mother-in-law?

I would show Gloria the stream of texts from my parents later. I knew she would crack up. My mother could not have been more excited. We weren't talking much in there; I couldn't concentrate, Gloria looked like she was in the same condition, and Tommy could obviously tell we were not going to be good for anything. Then the door in the back of the room opened, the celebrant stepped in and said "It's time," and suddenly I was laser focused.

I said, "See you in a minute, baby," and went out the side door into the chapel. Did we really know this many people? It was nothing like Salma and Gonzo's wedding (there they were, twisted around to see what was happening at the back, like everyone else), but it seemed like all the people in the world. I'm not sure I managed to smile at them. I looked up at the front. My parents were looking back at me with such love and pride I almost teared up. I took a deep breath, let it out slowly, took another and walked down the aisle.

Scott was standing to one side with his trumpet in hand, mute in place. The side door opened again. Scott lifted the instrument and started to play. *Oh my God*, I thought, almost cracking up. It was so fucking perfect. A fanfare, a salute, an announcement: here she comes, the queen of the day, the queen of my heart. Tommy led her through the door and I could tell she was biting back a guffaw. There was a rustle as everyone stood up. Scott played her down the aisle, ending with a flourish. Tommy gave her a kiss and went to stand beside Dawn. Everybody sat down.

"Dearly beloved," said the celebrant. I tried to listen, I really did. But I was holding Gloria's hands and this was the best day of my entire blessed life. I'm pretty sure I didn't mess up any of the responses, because nobody said anything about a do-over, but I'd have to see the video to know for sure.

Then there was a short break while Gino sang 'Love Me Tender,' and I'm positive almost everyone in the room was crying. I certainly was. Gloria was. She pulled out a bandanna after Gino sat down and blotted my face with it. I noticed it was printed with playing cards. I took it out of her hand and returned the favor. Once we were all composed again, it was time for the rings.

You would think this was something we would have discussed. It's part of the ceremony, after all. But we weren't writing our own vows or anything like that. Gloria spoke to the organizer about our music, and I had a word with her about the fact we weren't having any readings or speeches, and that was it. Gloria hadn't asked about rings. A few months back I volunteered the fact that I was getting her one. She nodded in a sort of 'aha I thought so' way and changed the subject. She did not say she was getting me one, and I didn't mention it. But this was the woman who got me flowers for Valentine's Day, so I was not completely surprised when, after I slid the new platinum band onto her finger and replaced her engagement ring beside it, she put her right hand in her pocket and pulled something out. "With this ring I thee wed," she said, and took my big hand in both of hers. The ring was platinum like hers, satin finish with shiny edges that looked like the metal was braided. Simple, solid, and significant. It looked good on my hand. "Don't you ever take this off." I glanced up from our hands to her face; she was grinning at me.

"Not a chance," I said.

"Then seal these vows with a kiss," suggested the celebrant, and boy did we ever. There was applause. When I finally let go of Gloria, she got that bandanna out again and wiped the lipstick off my face.

Everyone knew we were heading out more or less immediately, so the only people who followed us down the aisle and into the side room were our parents and the celebrant. We finished the paperwork in a few minutes, did the hugs and kisses. Then two more people came in: my pilot friend Bob and his wife Edie. Bob said, "You're not going to McCarran. I'm taking you to Cabo."

Then there was the capper. Edie said, "Mr. Corsetti has a limo for you. We'll head over now and see you there."

Gloria said, "Holy shit! Really?! That's awesome!" Our parents all cracked up. Bob and Edie took off, there was another round of kisses and hugs and handshakes, and not too much later Gloria looked at me and said, "Is it time?"

I thought it probably was. I got my phone out and texted Scott: *Were you in on this travel plan?*

He must have been waiting. *Gino texted me this morning. Your bags are already in the limo*

Thanks buddy. Have fun at the ranch with Kathy this weekend

LOL I plan to. See you Monday

Gloria was waiting none-too-patiently, so I put the phone away. "Now it's time, baby." I offered my arm; she linked hers through it; we strolled through the exit door like people who had someplace to be.

XV – Gloria

September 2016

You would think I would be all jaded about the private-plane, limo driver, whatever kind of deal by now. I was not. I was not any more used to luxurious travel (and for the record, Bob's plane was not some gold-plated thing, it was simply not a low-cost cattle car) than I was to being on stage with Gino Corsetti every night. I only managed not to fully sob while he was singing by biting hard on the inside of my lip. I ran my tongue over that now and said, "He is actually the best boss in the world, right? It isn't my imagination."

Lou said, "It isn't your imagination. Are you going to make any kind of announcement on Tuesday?"

I blinked. I hadn't even thought of it. But Gino made kind of a production out of his anniversary in April, he'd made kind of a production out of it when Sergei proposed, and if he wasn't actually expecting me to say anything he also probably didn't mind. Then I snorted out a laugh because of course the next thing I thought of was what could we play, and the answer was 'Love and Marriage.' A hit for Frank Sinatra, and one that had such a pop-culture hook thanks to that TV show. Then there was 'Makin' Whoopee.' I was mentally flipping through the fake book. There were so many appropriate songs, and so many more that would be hilariously inappropriate. We couldn't make the whole set about me, of course. I sent a text to Gino and decided to forget about it. Monday night was early enough to get back to those questions. "So I wanted to thank you for keeping your high-school class ring somewhere I could snag it and take it to the jeweler.

And also for putting it on that time so I knew it still fit you."

Lou was smiling at me. If he were the sneaky type I'd think he did both those things deliberately. Actually, now that I thought about it, he *was* the sneaky type. My engagement ring, the record player, that first casual suggestion about flying to Santa Fe. That reminded me I needed to text Grandma. I was still doing that when we got to the air strip. The check-in process was a little more involved this time since we were crossing the border, but it was still so much easier than commercial flight. We double-checked that we had all our crap and headed out onto the tarmac. Bob and Edie were both there. The look on Edie's face made me ask, "Oh, are you coming along? Going to have your own dirty weekend?"

"There are reasons to make this a leisure flight," she said. "And I haven't been to Cabo for ages."

"Well let's get on board. Look what Gino sent along in the limo." I brandished the bottle of chilled champagne.

"Jesus, Glory, don't shake that." Lou was cracking up. He and Bob got the bags up the stairs (Lou took the champagne too) and then came back down to supervise while Edie and I went up. She said she'd be in the cockpit with Bob till after takeoff, then join us in the main cabin.

"I was thinking," Lou said as we got settled, "You should wear this outfit next time you go to the Grammys. You look like a movie star."

"Aw, Lou. The dress turned out good, huh?"

"It's fantastic. Did you wish you had a veil?"

"Oh my *God* I totally did! All those people staring at me! Did you wish you had one?"

He was laughing. "I totally did. What did Grandma say?"

"She said Dad did a great job holding the phone steady for FaceTime except when Gino was singing. And she'll see us at Christmas." There was a lot more than that, of course, but I could show him the text exchange later. "I kind of felt like my parents might not be such a disaster from here on out."

"I thought so too. Mom texted a million times this morning and she said they're all going to have dinner again tonight."

"Good," I said, surprised. "Great. You know what this means?"

"What, honey."

"It means our wedding did what a wedding is supposed to do. Turned two families into one family. That isn't even why I wanted to marry you but it's kind of a fucking great side-effect, isn't it?"

"Yes it is." He was smiling against my mouth. I let him kiss me for a while. I never bothered freshening up my lipstick after the ceremony. Time enough for that when we got to the airport in Cabo.

We went into the airport café with Bob and Edie for lunch, thanked them about a thousand times, and confirmed the rendezvous time for getting our asses back to Las Vegas on Monday. Between me and Edie, Lou hadn't gotten much of the champagne, and of course poor Bob didn't have a drop. He said they were heading straight to a hotel with a swim-up bar. I looked at Lou and demanded to know if our hotel had a swim-up bar. He said, "Would I take you someplace that didn't?"

"Of course not. I should know better. You are, in hotel-booking as in everything else, perfect." He kissed me again, there went the lipstick again, and then we went to find our ground transportation.

If you've never been to Cabo I strongly recommend it. Possibly not at spring break, but September was a good time to go. There may be all kinds of interesting activities provided for non-honeymooners. These honeymooners were providing their own interesting activities. We ate mass quantities of fresh seafood, drank like it was about to be outlawed, screwed with gusto, and wore the absolute minimum of clothing.

While wearing minimal clothing, in between the other things, I kept up with entertainment news in general and with Vegas news in particular. The new season of 'Behind the Strip' was going into production in October. Now that Ruben and Oscar and I had our groove for the scoring, I wasn't at all nervous about fitting that in. I looked up the date the Grammy nominations were supposed to be announced, and put that in my calendar. The second single was doing really well, and so was the 'Hit Me' remix. Last year I didn't even have the nominations on my radar. Now, with three hits from the new album, I couldn't help hoping.

Dad texted to say his 'Thief of Hearts' jam session with Ruben and Oscar went great. They recorded a dirty demo to play me when I was back in town. I told my husband (how much did I love using that word?) about it while we were lounging by the pool.

"What does that mean, dirty demo." Lou sounded lazy, or buzzed, or both.

"It means they took it somewhere with lousy acoustics, on lousy equipment. It's only so a person can get an idea whether what they're doing is worth working on. Wouldn't be surprised if they took it in the green room with somebody's phone."

"That must have been a hassle for Ruben."

"You'd be surprised how fast he can set up and break down the drums. But he had to set up for the show anyway." I patted Lou's thigh. Let my fingertips rest on the scar. "This feels hot. I'm going to put some sunscreen on it." That new skin was still a little tender. Which made it a particularly effective place to put my mouth. Maybe Lou was thinking the same thing; his trunks had more of a bulge than usual. You would think with the amount of screwing we were doing, it would take more than that. You would be wrong.

"Or we could go inside," he suggested. "We can always come back out later."

"This is true." It was late afternoon on Sunday; we had almost twenty-four hours of honeymoon left. With that in mind, I stroked up the inside of his thigh, watching the bulge. He caught my hand, laughing, then sat up, leaned over to kiss me, and swung his legs off the lounger. He scooped his towel up, doing a quick wrap around his waist. I organized myself and followed him off the pool deck.

As it happened, we didn't go back out later. Clouds rolled in, bringing a thoroughly awesome thunderstorm. We sat on the little balcony of our room, barely inside the dry zone, watching the lightning out at sea, holding hands. We were drinking decaf from the room's coffeemaker with rum from the mini-bar and half-seriously discussing going downstairs for dinner in the restaurant, versus getting room service again. "Oh the hell with it," I said. "I like our view up here."

"Me too," Lou said, looking at me. "I'm going to like this view for the rest of my life."

My hair was a disaster, I had no makeup on, was just this side of sunburned, and definitely needed a shower. Of course, all those also applied to Lou except the thing about the hair. He did need a shave, though.

"I love you so much," I said, setting down my coffee cup. "What should the next album be?"

"I love you so much, too. After 'Thief of Hearts?'"

I nodded. He didn't even hesitate. "Elvis."

He read my mind again. I had to warn him, though. "You know that means I won't have to spend my vacation writing songs."

"Guess we'll just have to do something else." He lifted our joined hands to his lips. The lines around his eyes crinkled with a smile.

God, you're gorgeous, I thought. "Guess so. Could you arrange to not have some new kind of cheater fucking around in your high-rollers room next summer?"

"I'll see what I can do."

"And also whatever's happening with the music village must be in condition to do without your attention for a couple of weeks."

He was laughing silently. He kissed my knuckles again and let go of my hand. "Do I need to do something else with your mouth right now?"

"I think you do." I leaned over to kiss him. "Husband."

"Wife." He got his hand under my chair and pulled it closer.

"Goddamn, you're strong."

Then that hand was in my hair and he was kissing me again, and I stopped thinking of anything else.

THE END

If you enjoyed A WINNING HAND, please consider leaving a positive rating or review. It really helps! Thanks for reading.

Want more? **TODAY, TOMORROW & FOREVER** and **TAKE A NOTE** feature more characters involved with 'Behind the Strip.' Discover this world of romance at www.thelastories.com.

****

About the Author

Alexandra Caluen lives in a small purple house with her husband, a bottle of Laphroaig, a lot of books, and nine pairs of ballroom shoes. She works in patent law and has enough hair for three people.